ACCEPTING
MR. DARCY

A Pride and Prejudice Variation

Jane Grix

Jane Grix

Cover design by beetifulbookcovers.com
Cover image by id1974/depositphotos.com
Formatting by Polgarus Studio

To learn about new books and short stories by Jane Grix, sign up for her mailing list at: www.janegrix.com

PROLOGUE

"Dearly beloved, we are gathered here in the sight of God, and in the face of this congregation, to join together this Man and this Woman in holy Matrimony. . ."

Elizabeth Bennet tried to listen to the words of the marriage ceremony, but her thoughts were racing. Was it a sin to marry a man she did not love?

She glanced briefly at her future husband, Mr. Darcy, who looked solemn, if not stern in his wedding finery.

He caught her looking at him and his expression softened a little and she looked down quickly.

". . . and therefore is not by any to be enterprised, nor taken in hand, unadvisedly, lightly, or wantonly . . ."

She certainly had not made this decision lightly, however quickly she had agreed to it, and in the three weeks since Mr. Darcy's proposal at Hunsford, she had ample opportunity to rescind her agreement, if she had chosen.

Was it unadvised? Charlotte had not thought so. From the beginning she had encouraged her to pay more attention to Mr. Darcy than to Mr. Wickham.

"*. . . considering the causes for which Matrimony was ordained. First, it was ordained for the procreation of children. . .*"

Children. Elizabeth had always wanted to marry someday and to have children, but now those children would be Mr. Darcy's, and in order to bear those children, she would have to allow him the physical liberties that her mother had explained so bluntly the night before. Having occasionally seen animals copulating, Elizabeth supposed it was biologically necessary, but it seemed such an awkward and potentially embarrassing process. But she would try not to think of that now. First she had to get through the ceremony and the wedding breakfast without disgracing herself. She must pretend to be happy.

"*. . .Therefore, if any man can shew any just cause, why they may not lawfully be joined together, let him now speak, or else hereafter for ever hold his peace. . .*"

Elizabeth held her breath, hoping against hope that someone would speak up and stop her from doing what she was doing.

The minister continued in a solemn tone, "I require and charge you both, as ye will answer at the dreadful day of judgment when the secrets of all hearts may be disclosed, that if either of you know any impediment, why ye may not be lawfully joined together in Matrimony, ye do now confess it."

Elizabeth shivered. God knew the state of her heart and the lie she was about to give.

The minister turned to Mr. Darcy. "Fitzwilliam James Darcy, Wilt thou have this woman to thy wedded wife, to live together after God's ordinance in the holy estate of matrimony? Wilt thou love her, comfort her, honour, and keep her in sickness and in health; and forsaking all others, keep thee only unto her, so long as you both shall live?"

"I will." Mr. Darcy's voice seemed deeper than usual.

The minister turned to her. "Elizabeth Francis Bennet, wilt thou have this man to thy wedded husband, to live together after God's ordinance in the holy estate of matrimony? Wilt thou obey him . . ."

Obey was such a frightening word, and for a moment she did not hear the rest of the sentence, and then she saw that everyone was waiting for her response. She had heard the ceremony dozens of times. She knew what she was agreeing to, but a more important question was how could she keep her vows?

"I will," she said quietly.

The ceremony continued, and her father acknowledged that he was giving her away. He looked at her briefly, as if noting her concerns, then smiled grimly. He had never specifically mentioned it, but she knew him well enough to know that he knew her reasons for accepting Mr. Darcy.

Mr. Darcy took her right hand in his right hand and repeated the words of the troth.

Then it was her turn. She stumbled over the words "to have and to hold from this day forward" and by the end of the sentence her voice was no louder than a whisper.

But it was loud enough to count. Mr. Darcy said solemnly, "With this ring, I thee wed, with my body I thee worship, and with all my worldly goods I thee endow. . ."

Elizabeth flushed, knowing that this was the crux of the matter. She was marrying Mr. Darcy for his money.

She hoped that in doing so she hadn't damned her soul to hell.

They both knelt and the vicar continued, quoting scripture and giving them advice. It seemed to take forever, but then before she was ready, it was over.

Once they were outside, someone cried, "Kiss the bride."

Mr. Darcy's eyes met hers. He looked pleased, and she felt as if she might faint.

Elizabeth steeled herself. I can do this, she thought desperately. I have to do this. She made herself smile and lifted her chin as he bent his head lower to hers and their lips met.

CHAPTER ONE

SEVEN WEEKS EARLIER

Elizabeth knocked on the library door at Longbourn and thought she heard her father say, "Come in," so she opened the door and stepped inside.

But her father startled. He was lying on a couch with a damp cloth on his forehead. His face was pale, but he sat up quickly when he saw her. "Forgive me," he said pleasantly and set the cloth aside. "I must have been taking a nap."

"Perhaps Cowper has put you to sleep," she joked, seeing the volume on the floor beside him.

He smiled, but then he winced and put a hand on his side, near his waist. "I must have a stitch," he said quickly, not meeting her eyes.

She was alarmed. "Truly sir, you look ill. Would you like me to get something for you? A glass of wine perhaps?"

He shook his head. "A new stomach perhaps?" he said, then added, "But that would never work. With my luck, I would receive a stomach like Sir William Lucas."

Sir William, one of their closest neighbours, was a rotund gentleman whose waistcoat buttons always seemed to be on the brink of bursting. She saw now that her father was thin, almost frail, and his skin had a yellow cast. His clothing seemed too large and hung on him. Why had she not noticed this before or had the changes been so gradual that she had not paid attention? "Are you ill?"

He looked at her, as if debating whether to tell another joke, but then he admitted, "Yes. I am. I have been ill the past few months, but do not tell your mother. She would only fret, and I would rather my last days not be filled with her histrionics."

"Last days?" Elizabeth repeated in alarm. "Surely not. Have you spoken with Mr. Jones?"

"Yes, and two other physicians besides. I am dying, Lizzy."

Elizabeth put her hand to her mouth, trying not to cry. "Then I will not go to Hunsford to visit the Collinses. I will stay at home."

"No," Mr. Bennet said. "I want you to go. Jane has gone to London and you need your trip as well. There will be time enough to grieve when I am actually dead. Right now I want you to enjoy yourself. Although I am not certain how enjoyable it will be to spend four weeks listening to Mr. Collins at the dinner table. I believe three days would be my limit for the man."

Elizabeth said, "Is there nothing you can do to feel better?"

"No, I have a growth in my stomach, and my days are numbered."

Thinking back, Elizabeth realized that her father had been eating little at meals and for the past few months he had spent even more time in the library. She had thought he was merely trying to avoid Kitty and Lydia's youthful exuberance, but she supposed he had been hiding his symptoms. He continued, "But be of good cheer. I do believe I shall last until you return. If not, know that I love you dearly. You are a good girl, and I regret that I was not able to see you happily settled."

"Perhaps I should have accepted Mr. Collins after all," she said dryly, which made him smile weakly.

"I said 'happily settled,'" Mr. Bennet reminded. "And I had hoped that your sister Jane might end up with Mr. Bingley, but that came to nought."

Mr. Bingley was a wealthy young gentleman who had moved to their village a few months before, renting Netherfield Park, a large neighbouring manor house. He had seemed besotted with her older sister Jane, but after hosting a ball, he had gone to London, never to return. His sister wrote, saying that he did not intend to return to Hertfordshire, and Elizabeth did not know what to think. She feared that Mr. Bingley's haughty sisters had convinced him to stay away.

"Has Jane met Mr. Bingley in London?" Mr. Bennet asked.

"No, sir," Elizabeth said. After Christmas Jane had gone to visit their Aunt and Uncle Gardiner in Cheapside.

"That is too bad, for I have never seen her happier than when he was around. But it does not matter. For the financial security of our family, I would have preferred at least one of you to marry a wealthy man, but Mr. Gardiner will take you in when Mr. Collins throws you out."

Mr. Collins, a clergyman, was Mr. Bennet's distant cousin and the heir to Longbourn. For years her mother had said she could not stand the man and often railed against the entailment that made her husband's property pass directly to a male heir. But the autumn before he had visited and had proposed to Elizabeth, winning Mrs. Bennet's favour. Mrs. Bennet had been very angry when Elizabeth refused him and even more furious when their friend Charlotte Lucas married him instead.

Since then, Mrs. Bennet often said, "Lizzy, it will be all your fault when he throws us into the hedgerows once your father is dead."

Mrs. Bennet had no idea how soon that might be.

Elizabeth could tell that her father was comforted by the thought that Mr. Gardiner would make all things well. But from a few comments Jane had let slip into her letters, Elizabeth did not think that her Uncle Gardiner's business was thriving. This trip there had been no mention of shopping excursions or trips to the theatre. Elizabeth remembered her Aunt Gardiner's comments at Christmas about Mr. Wickham. She had warned Elizabeth about the imprudence of falling in love with a man who could not support her. "Love has its place, but you must be able to pay for coal." Elizabeth wondered now if her aunt's advice had been based on personal experience. Elizabeth asked her father, "Will there be any funds, other than what was settled on my mother?" At his death her mother would receive five thousand pounds, and the interest on that sum would not be enough to support their family.

"Hardly enough to signify. I'm sorry Lizzy. At first your mother and I thought we would have a son, and by the time we realized that none were coming, it was too late to economize. I have done what I could, but your mother and sisters have extravagant tastes, and I did not have the will to check them." Mr. Bennet sighed. "I am afraid I have been a poor father."

He was a good man but ineffectual. Rather than lead his family in wisdom, he had been content sit back and laugh at their follies. Elizabeth had often wished that he would take command, but it had not been her place to school him. And she loved him too much to make him feel worse now. "I love you, Father," she said simply.

"Come give me a kiss," he ordered, tapping his cheek with one finger. "Then go finish your packing."

"Yes, sir," she said, obeying him.

She walked up to her bedroom in a sombre frame of mind.

Her father was dying. In a few months, he would be gone, and what would become of them if her Uncle Gardiner could not take them in? Her Aunt and Uncle Philips who lived nearby in Meryton would probably take her mother and possibly Lydia, but they did not have sufficient room for all six of them, even if there were sufficient funds to feed them, which she doubted. Aunt Philips was like her mother, enthralled with fripperies, and from what Elizabeth had overheard in the past few years, her aunt's expenses often outran the family income.

Oh dear, Elizabeth thought. Only yesterday she had been thinking it was time to buy new dancing shoes because hers were worn. But now there would be no need, for she would not dance while she was in mourning.

As Elizabeth thought of her father dying, she cried a little, then washed her face and put on a brave smile. At least his death would not take her by surprise, and she had a few weeks, possibly longer, to plan.

For a few minutes she wished that she was a man. Men in financial straits could find employment. They could study the law or become a soldier like Mr. Wickham. Intellectually she was qualified to be a clerk or assistant for someone in business, but as a woman she had few options. Seamstresses and maids hardly made any money at all. She might possibly be able to support herself by becoming a governess or a paid companion, but she would not be able to earn enough to help her four sisters.

The only solution was the one she liked the least: she must marry a man with money.

The difficulty was that the only single young men of fortune she knew were Mr. Bingley, Jane's potential beau, and his friend Mr. Darcy. Unfortunately Mr. Darcy was a proud, disagreeable man. He had come down to visit his friend Bingley a few months before and spent several weeks at Netherfield, an estate only three miles from Longbourn.

She had met him first at an assembly at Meryton. She had found him much more handsome than Mr. Bingley, but he did not have his friend's happy manners. He was aloof and condescending, too good for his company. And he had a way of looking down at her as if he found something at fault. She had overheard him say that she was not pretty.

Normally she would have laughed off the slight. Why should she care what he thought of her? He was nothing to her.

But there was something about him that she could not resist. She liked irritating him, seeing if she could make his eyes flash or those stern brows furrow. It had been a game to her.

They had briefly shared a house when Jane was ill and visiting at Netherfield. In those few days she had the opportunity to see him interact with his friends in more casual settings and he had been equally annoying. When he spoke, he was often stiff, speaking as if he was lecturing to an ignorant crowd. He acted as if his opinion was the only reasonable one. It was infuriating.

Soon afterward, she had learned that he had ruined the fortunes of Mr. Wickham by refusing to honour a bequest in his late father's will. At that point Elizabeth's dislike of Mr. Darcy had grown even deeper. She knew it was natural for men of wealth to ignore the misfortunes of others, but he had actually harmed Mr. Wickham.

In sharp contrast to Mr. Darcy, Mr. Wickham was the most pleasant, the most interesting man she had met in years. At first she thought he liked her as much as she liked him, but he had recently become engaged to a local heiress. She did not judge him. She supposed he was only being prudent, as she now must be as well.

Elizabeth sighed. If only there was a way to find a man with Mr. Darcy's wealth, Mr. Wickham's charm, and the body of Mr. Higgins' eldest son. Mr. Higgins was one of her father's tenants and the year before she had seen his eldest son working in the fields. The man had removed his shirt, displaying a physique that would put some of the Greek marble statues to shame. Even now, Elizabeth blushed to remember it.

Elizabeth laughed at herself. The possibility of finding an ideal man was a slim one. With her luck, she was more likely to end up with a man with Mr. Wickham's money, Mr. Darcy's charm, and Sir William Lucas' body.

* * *

On the way to Hunsford, Elizabeth, Sir William and Charlotte's sister Maria stopped at Gracechurch Street in London. Elizabeth had been invited to travel with Charlotte's relations on their visit. Elizabeth was pleased to see Jane again, but she noticed that her Aunt Gardiner seemed unusually harried. She was a gracious hostess, and the dinner meal lacked nothing, but the next day, there was no shopping and no trip to the theatre. Sir William took Maria to see some sites by hackney and asked Elizabeth if she wished to go as well.

Elizabeth declined, saying that she wished to spend time with Jane instead.

"Jane, tell me everything," she said when they were alone. "How fares our aunt and uncle?"

Jane bit her lip. "I do not know exactly. We rarely see Uncle Gardiner. He seems very occupied with his business."

Just as she had feared. When the business was thriving, Mr. Gardiner was an excellent host, constantly suggesting excursions and treats to make their visits memorable. "And Aunt Gardiner?"

"She appreciates my help with the children. But she is with child again, and I think that wearies her."

If the Gardiners were expecting another child, that was yet another reason why they should not have to take in her entire family. "Have you heard more from Miss Bingley?"

"No. She only called that once, and I wrote you about that."

Elizabeth nodded. Miss Bingley had made a perfunctory morning visit and had left as quickly as possible. Elizabeth did not want to say anything more about the Bingleys. From the way Jane looked away, Elizabeth knew she was thinking about Bingley and she did not want to say his name, causing her more sorrow.

The next day they drove on to Hunsford. When Elizabeth arrived, she was met by Mr. Collins and Charlotte. Marriage had given her friend dignity and status, although at what a cost. Mr. Collins was as foolish as he had been before. He was overly polite, a strange mixture of humility and self-importance. He gave Elizabeth a tour of the house and garden, pointing out all the finer aspects, including their view of Rosings Park, the home of Lady Catherine de Bourgh, Mr. Collin's patroness. During the tour, Elizabeth often glanced at Charlotte, wondering how she could bear to live with this man, but that was one question she would not ask.

Within the first two days of her visit, they were invited to dine with Lady Catherine. Elizabeth looked forward to the event, if only to be able to report back to her father. Lady Catherine was even more than she had expected. She was a tall, strong willed woman with a fierce expression. She monopolized the conversation, and from some of the particulars, it was clear that she took an avid interest in the running of the parsonage. Poor Charlotte, Elizabeth thought more than once. Not only are you married to Mr. Collins, you have to endure his employer as well. But other than blushing a few times, Charlotte seemed to be unmoved. She spent many hours every day in her garden and her sitting room, seemingly happy with her domestic comforts.

You are a better woman than I am, Elizabeth thought. If she married a man as irritating as Mr. Collins, she thought she would go mad or be inspired to violence.

After one week, Sir William returned to Hertfordshire, leaving Elizabeth and Maria behind. A few days later, Elizabeth was alarmed to learn that Mr. Darcy would be visiting along with his cousin Colonel Fitzwilliam. Apparently they both came to Rosings every spring. Elizabeth did not look forward to seeing Mr. Darcy again, but she did think it might be interesting to observe Mr. Darcy with his cousin, Miss Anne de Bourgh. Wickham had said that they would marry someday. She wondered how that stern, superior man could wish to marry his cousin, who was frail and sickly, without ten words to say for herself. But Elizabeth supposed he might not care. Miss de Bourgh was the heir of Rosings, and Mr. Darcy struck her as a man who cared for wealth and position. She did feel some sympathy for Miss de Bourgh, though. She pitied any young woman who would have to love, cherish and obey Mr. Darcy.

* * *

Darcy was at the dinner table with Lady Catherine and his cousins Miss Anne and Colonel Fitzwilliam when his aunt mentioned the visitors at the Parsonage. "Mrs. Collins has a sister visiting and a young woman friend from Hertfordshire."

Darcy felt a frisson of disquiet. "Perhaps I have met the young woman. I was visiting my friend Mr. Bingley in the autumn and met several people from the town where Mrs. Collins lived."

Lady Catherine said, "Yes, Mrs. Collins assures me that you have met. Her name is Miss Bennet."

Please, let it be her older sister Jane, Mr. Darcy thought.

"Elizabeth Bennet," Lady Catherine continued. "She is a well-formed girl with passable piano skills. But she is pert."

That was one way to describe her, he thought. But to him, Elizabeth Bennet was brilliant, beautiful and clever. Back in Hertfordshire he had come close to making a cake of himself. If it were not for her low connections – multiple extended family members in trade — and her vulgar mother, he might have been tempted to offer for her. He had been relieved to leave Hertfordshire and was determined to avoid Meryton forever.

"There is nothing I like better than a pert young woman," Colonel Fitzwilliam said cheerfully. "Does she have a fortune?"

"Nothing to signify," Lady Catherine said. "I have heard from Mr. Collins that her dowry will be something along the lines of a thousand pounds."

The Colonel sighed. "Not enough."

"No. That would hardly keep you in neck cloths," Darcy joked. He smiled, but he did not like the idea of his cousin courting Elizabeth Bennet. For once he was glad that his cousin was a second son without a large income.

"Yes," Lady Catherine agreed. "She will be unlikely to find any gentleman willing to marry her. I am surprised that she did not marry her cousin Mr. Collins when she had the opportunity."

"Mr. Collins?" Darcy said. Her obnoxious cousin? "What is this?"

Lady Catherine was happy to explain. "A few months ago, Mr. Collins visited Longbourn. I know he wanted to research the extent of his future inheritance, but he also went with a plan of marrying one of the daughters. I told him it was time to settle down. I believe clergymen should be married. I told him to choose properly, to choose a gentlewoman for my sake and for his own, I recommended that the young woman be an active, useful sort of person, not brought up high, but able to make small income go a good way."

Darcy was still dumbfounded. He supposed in some ways Elizabeth Bennet would meet that criteria, but she was so much more. And she deserved more than to be legshackled to her idiot cousin. He said carefully, "Did Mr. Collins propose to her?"

"Yes. It is unbelievable, but true. She rejected him, saying that she would not make him happy." Lady Catherine shook her head at this foolishness. "Marriage is not merely a matter of happiness. It is an obligation, an investment."

Darcy was not surprised by her statement. From what he had observed, his aunt's marriage to Sir Lewis de Bourgh had been a formal one, based primarily on rank and position. He had never seen either of them express a kind or tender gesture. His parents, in contrast, had cared for each other. His father had been extremely grieved when his mother died. For more than a year, he seemed to lose all interest in life, but eventually the obligations of Pemberley had revived him.

Lady Catherine continued. "Young people today read too much poetry. They have unreasonable expectations."

Darcy thought back to a conversation he'd had with Elizabeth Bennet. She had joked about one sonnet killing a love outright. She had a clever, analytical way of viewing the world. She was not a simpering miss, easily persuaded by flowery compliments. The man who won her hand would have to earn it.

"Perhaps Miss Bennet is in love with another," the Colonel said.

Darcy was uncomfortable by the course the conversation was taking. He remembered the last time he spoke with Elizabeth. She had asked him about Mr. Wickham. Darcy clenched his teeth. It infuriated him to see the way Wickham had wormed his way into the good graces of Meryton. Had he wormed his way into Elizabeth's heart as well? Was she in love with him?

Lady Catherine said, "Then she was a fool to let her affection keep her from securing a husband. She may never receive another offer of marriage."

"I doubt that," Mr. Darcy said hotly, then clamped his lips shut, wishing he had kept his own counsel.

"Why?" the Colonel asked. "Is she pretty?"

"Yes," Darcy said shortly.

Lady Catherine looked up at him, her eyes narrowing with suspicion.

Darcy looked down and busied himself with deboning the pheasant on his plate.

Colonel Fitzwilliam said, "Good. Then I look forward to meeting her, even if I will not be offering her marriage."

* * *

Charlotte hurried into the sitting room to speak to Elizabeth. "Mr. Collins has returned from Rosings and it appears he has brought both Mr. Darcy and his cousin. I saw them from the window and they will be here in a moment." She hastily tucked a loose strand of hair into her lace cap and sat down, her hands clasped gently in her lap.

Elizabeth set aside the shirt she was hemming and prepared herself to meet their guests as well. She smoothed the skirt of her morning dress and tried to smile.

"I believe you are the reason for this civility," Charlotte whispered. "Mr. Darcy would never have come so soon to wait upon me."

Elizabeth shook her head at this foolishness but said

nothing for fear that it might be overheard. Charlotte liked to tease her, hinting that Mr. Darcy found her attractive or that he wanted to spend time with her. Her friend found it particularly persuasive that Elizabeth had been the only woman Mr. Darcy had asked to dance at the Netherfield Ball at the end of November. "And you know how much he despises dancing, Lizzy," Charlotte had said at the time. "I think he likes you."

Well, Elizabeth thought when the brief morning visit was over, if Mr. Darcy did like her, he had a strange way of showing it. He had been just as he seemed in Hertfordshire: reserved and stiff, meeting only the barest minimums of civility. He paid his compliments to Mrs. Collins and asked herself about the health of her family. Other than that, he held himself silent and aloof, which made her wonder why he had made the effort to come at all.

Colonel Fitzwilliam, on the other hand, was a much more promising gentleman. He talked very pleasantly. He did not have his cousin's good looks, but in person and address was a complete gentleman. He was about thirty years of age, well-dressed, with well-bred manners. Elizabeth wondered if he had an income. He was a soldier, but many young men of quality went into the army. She looked forward to getting to know him better.

In the next week Lady Catherine kept her guests to herself. The Colonel called at the parsonage more than once, but Mr. Darcy they only saw at church, which was fine with Elizabeth. She was able to pay attention to Mr. Collin's sermon and other than brief nods in greeting when they left the church, she had been able to ignore Mr. Darcy completely.

She began to think that his presence in Kent would not bother her at all, but then they were asked to visit Lady Catherine Sunday evening. "What generosity, what condescension," Mr. Collins said. "I did not think Lady Catherine would invite us when she had visitors in the house, but she has. I can hardly contain my joy at the prospect."

And I can hardly contain my irritation, Elizabeth thought. As much as she would not mind speaking with Colonel Fitzwilliam, she did not want to spend an evening with Mr. Darcy glaring at her across the room.

When they entered Lady Catherine's drawing room, the Colonel appeared to be the only person who was sincerely glad to see them. Lady Catherine was barely civil and was engrossed with her nephews, speaking primarily to them, especially to Darcy.

Darcy looked particularly fine in his evening dress with his tall starched collar and brilliant cravat drawing her eye to his handsome countenance and square jaw. His attire was everything proper: immaculate without ostentation. She guessed that the bill for his laundry alone would be more than what her entire family spent for clothing. But clothing, however fine, did not make the man. She much preferred Colonel Fitzwilliam.

The Colonel sat next to Elizabeth and they talked of travel, new books, and music. Elizabeth thought that she had never been so well entertained. She felt a little disloyal to think that she was enjoying the Colonel's company more than she had enjoyed Wickham's. But that was foolishness. Wickham was engaged to another. He had not thought of her, so she should not think of him, not even to make comparisons.

Lady Catherine saw that they were talking and interrupted. "What is it you are talking of?" she demanded. "Let me hear what it is."

"We are speaking of music," the Colonel said.

"Of music!" she exclaimed. "I am most interested in the subject." She took over the conversation, praising her own taste and musical talents, which she had not developed. She mentioned Anne, who looked embarrassed, and then asked Darcy about his sister Georgiana and her progress on the pianoforte.

Darcy answered civilly, but Elizabeth could tell

from the way his jaw was clenched that he was irritated by his aunt.

"She must practise every day," Lady Catherine said. "And so should you, Miss Bennet. You have not had the benefit of tutors on the same level as Georgiana, but that does not mean you cannot improve yourself by a strict regimen of daily practise. I know that Mrs. Collins does not have an instrument, so you should come to Rosings. In fact, I insist upon it. Mr. Collins, will you make certain your guest comes to Rosings daily to practise?"

"Yes, ma'am."

"I hate to think of any young woman wasting her potential."

Elizabeth sputtered, then strove to hide it with a discrete cough behind her hand. She glanced at the Colonel who appeared amused by the conversation and at Mr. Darcy who looked a little ashamed of his aunt's overbearing manner. She said finally. "You are too kind, but I would rather not. I would not want to bother you, ma'am, with my noise."

"Oh, that is no problem." Lady Catherine dismissed her concerns with a wave of her hand. "You may play the piano-forte in Mrs. Jenkinson's room. You will be in nobody's way in that part of the house."

Elizabeth did not know how to answer. Fortunately

the coffee arrived, interrupting the conversation. She glanced once at Mr. Darcy, wondering what he made of his aunt's commands, but she could not catch his eye.

* * *

Darcy sipped the dark liquid in his cup. Elizabeth Bennet was a breath of fresh air in his aunt's house. She was so lovely, so clever with a spark of humour in her eyes. He thought she was considerably patient with the rude, intrusive enquiries from his aunt. She was more courageous than either his cousin Anne or his sister Georgiana. Both of those young women turned into silent mice around Lady Catherine. He doubted that anyone would be able to intimidate Elizabeth. That was another of her traits that he admired – her ability to speak her mind without being shrill.

The man who married her would have a lifetime of intelligent conversation.

Colonel Fitzwilliam reminded Elizabeth of having promised to play for him, so she walked over to the pianoforte. Darcy didn't like the fact that they had promises between them, even if they were so inconsequential, because it showed that Elizabeth was more comfortable with his cousin than with him.

He watched as she walked across the room. Her

gown was a lovely shade of red, trimmed with gold ribbons. Her glorious dark hair was styled in curls upon her head and her throat was bare. She had a pleasing figure and a natural grace that drew his eye, as well as his cousin's.

The man who married her would be able to claim her physical charms as well, but he did not want to dwell on that.

The Colonel drew a chair to sit near her. Darcy wished he had thought of that himself. He tried to attend to her playing, but his aunt persisted in talking loudly over the song. Eventually, he excused himself and walked away from his aunt and towards the pianoforte.

Elizabeth looked up at him. "Do you mean to frighten me, Mr. Darcy, by coming in all this state to hear me?"

He knew she was joking. "You cannot really believe that I wish to alarm you."

"Perhaps not, but I know how well your sister plays and I fear my feeble attempts will not meet with your approval."

"You play charmingly," the Colonel said.

Elizabeth smiled at him and Darcy frowned. He feared that his cousin was focusing on Elizabeth's beauty and forgetting her lack of fortune.

Elizabeth saw the frown and said, "I can see that you disagree."

"No, I appreciate your talents and enjoy listening to you play."

"But like your aunt you think I would benefit from some additional tutoring."

"In theory, everyone would benefit from additional tutoring."

"Very politic, Mr. Darcy," she said lightly. "You danced around my comment most skillfully. I suppose you agree that we all have talents or areas of our character that could be improved upon."

"Are you referring to me?" he asked, amused. "I know you are a studier of personalities and that I have been under your observation. No doubt you have seen my many flaws."

"False modesty," Elizabeth said coolly.

"Oh do tell," the Colonel said. "How would you improve upon my cousin?"

"I would never be so bold." Her eyes danced with mischief.

Darcy said, "No, tell me. What would you change, if you could?"

She looked at him seriously and Darcy had a moment of doubt, then she smiled at him, her fine eyes sparkling. "I would have you dance more, Mr. Darcy."

She was the most enchanting creature. At that moment, he wished he could dance with her, to take her in his arms and waltz her around the floor. Or better still, take her onto the balcony and kiss her.

But that would never do.

She would be shocked. His aunt would be horrified.

But he was sorely tempted.

She turned to his cousin. "When I first met Mr. Darcy, it was at a local ball. Gentlemen were scarce and more than one young lady was sitting down in want of a partner. And your cousin stood by himself, refusing to join in the activities."

The Colonel nodded. "He does not like to dance, that is true. I, on the other hand, love to dance."

"Perhaps I need tutoring," Darcy said, drawing her attention back to him. "Would you be willing to assist me?"

Her cheeks flushed and he felt a responding surge of warmth himself. "There is no one to provide music, Mr. Darcy. Any such lessons would have to be at a later date."

"I look forward to that," he said seriously.

"Don't believe him," the Colonel teased.

His aunt, wishing to take part in the conversation, called out, demanding to know what they were discussing.

"Darcy is thinking of taking dance instruction," the Colonel said loudly.

"Don't be ridiculous," Lady Catherine said. "You dance perfectly well, Darcy. You have played long enough, Miss Bennet. It is time for us to play cards instead."

Darcy saw the hint of smile on Elizabeth's lips and thought that yes, it would be best if they did play cards. She was much too attractive. Hopefully playing cards would distract him.

CHAPTER TWO

Elizabeth found the next few days strange. Both the Colonel and Mr. Darcy called often at the Parsonage. Charlotte teased Elizabeth, telling her that there seemed to be a competition between them, with each trying to gain her affections. "Don't be ridiculous," Elizabeth said, quoting Lady Catherine and mimicking her tone.

Charlotte hid a smile. "You refuse to see what is before you."

Elizabeth continued in her own voice. "The poor men are both bored to death at Rosings Park. They come here only to escape the monotony. And as for their competition, that is common among family members. I have often seen brothers tease each other. It means nothing."

Charlotte just shook her head. "I will not be surprised if you receive an offer of marriage before they leave."

Elizabeth laughed. "And I will be surprised if I do."

But in spite of her merriment, she did consider the matter. She knew that Mr. Darcy would never propose, so that left the Colonel. Could she marry him? As the son of an Earl, he must have some financial resources. Would they be enough to benefit her family?

When she went walking in the grounds at Rosings, she met Mr. Darcy several times. He did not have much to say. He also came by the Parsonage once, by himself, and found her alone. They spoke awkwardly for a few minutes before Charlotte returned from her errand. Elizabeth wondered briefly if he was trying to get to know her better. Was he trying to determine whether she would be a suitable wife for his cousin?

She hoped he would not ruin her chances by telling the Colonel all about her ill-bred family.

Then a few days before the two gentlemen were scheduled to leave, she met Colonel Fitzwilliam on one of her walks. He seemed delighted to see her. He told her that he liked to make a tour of the Park every year and asked if she wished to join him.

She was so relieved that he was not Mr. Darcy that she gladly took the Colonel's arm.

As they walked she asked if he and his cousin were planning to leave Kent on Saturday.

"Yes, if Darcy does not put it off again."

"That surprises me. He seems like a man more decisive in his plans."

"Yes, but something keeps him here."

Elizabeth did not know how to interpret this statement, then blushed when the Colonel added, "And I do not mind the delay. Not when the company is so pleasant."

"I know your aunt enjoys your visit."

"I was not speaking of my aunt," he said clearly.

Is this it? Elizabeth thought, catching her breath. Was the Colonel going to ask her to marry him? She thought it was too soon. They hardly knew each other and she had not made up her mind yet whether she could accept him.

But then he seemed to check himself. He smiled and said nothing for almost a minute. When he spoke again, it was to admire the grounds and the view of Rosings Park in the distance. "It is not as grand as Darcy's Pemberley, but it is a pretty sight, don't you think? I particularly like the rose garden."

Elizabeth agreed, relieved that she did not need to make a decision at that moment.

The Colonel continued. "I have an interest in architecture. I have a hobby of mentally redesigning the places I visit. Adding wings, changing the windows, that sort of thing. It is an amusement."

Elizabeth thought it ironic that a soldier could be interested in more domestic matters. "And how would you improve Rosings?"

"Trim the bushes that line the entrance. At present they dwarf the front door."

Elizabeth squinted, imagining the change. "That is an excellent idea."

"Thank you." He added, "One day I hope to have my own property and spend my efforts improving it, but I suppose I will have to wait until I marry my heiress to put some of my ideas into effect."

"Your heiress?" Elizabeth asked, startled. "Are you engaged, sir? I had not heard."

He smiled. "No. In fact, I have yet to meet the young woman."

"Then how do you know she will be an heiress?"

"Because I cannot marry otherwise."

Elizabeth said nothing, colouring at his words. She knew this was meant for her. Perhaps he had noticed her interest in him and this was his way to warn her off.

He sighed dramatically, "It is the curse of being a younger son. I cannot marry where I like."

Elizabeth was determined to keep the conversation lively rather than serious. "My mother has told me that it is just as easy to fall in love with a rich man as a poor one. I suppose it is the same for men as well."

"Then you believe in love matches?"

"And you do not?"

He shrugged. "I suppose it is all right for some, but I have seen too many marriages that started with love but did not last in love. I think calm, mutual respect is a better approach."

"You may be right," Elizabeth said, smiling to herself. Apparently all of Charlotte's predictions were for nought. She would have to find someone else to marry, but she was surprised that she was not unduly upset. Her interest in the Colonel had not been deep. He had been a possibility, nothing more. If he had proposed, she would have considered the option seriously and most likely accepted it. She sighed. Perhaps she would become a governess after all. Or she and Jane could start a school. But she did not want to think those depressing thoughts.

"Pray, tell me," she said in a light tone. "What is the usual price of an Earl's younger son these days? Unless the elder brother is very sickly, I suppose you would not ask above fifty thousand pounds."

The Colonel answered in the same style, and the subject dropped.

They walked more and she hardly paid attention to the topics of their idle conversation. But then he mentioned Miss Georgiana Darcy and she said two of her acquaintances knew her: Mrs. Hurst and Miss Bingley.

The Colonel said he had met Mr. Bingley and found him to be a pleasant man.

Pleasant but inconstant, Elizabeth thought, thinking of Jane. She said, "He and Mr. Darcy appear to be close friends."

"Yes, Darcy is probably the best friend he ever had."

Elizabeth looked at him questioningly. "Why would you say that? I assume Mr. Bingley has numerous friends."

"Yes, but Darcy watches out for him."

"In what way? Does Mr. Bingley need a keeper?"

"In matters of love, perhaps," the Colonel said. "Recently Mr. Darcy saved him from a most imprudent marriage."

Elizabeth's heart grew cold. He could only be referring to Jane. "Did Mr. Darcy give you the reasons for his interference?"

"There were some very strong objections against the lady."

Objections against her family were more likely. No one knowing Jane could doubt her superiority.

And to think that Darcy had engineered her heartache. Who was he to decide upon the wisdom of his friend's inclination? Who was he to determine and direct in what manner his friend was to be made happy? She was appalled by his conceit and officious interference.

She thought of Jane, sweet, biddable Jane who was at this moment suffering, all because of Mr. Darcy.

In her anger, she acknowledged that Mr. Bingley was at fault as well. How could he be so weak as to walk away from the most wonderful girl he had ever met?

Men. At that moment, Elizabeth despised them all. But she said, "What arts did he use to separate them?"

"He did not talk to me of his own arts," said the Colonel, smiling. "He only told me what I have told you. And in truth, Darcy did not say it was Bingley, I merely supposed that he was the gentleman referenced because of the time they spent together last summer. It is all conjecture."

"Oh, if it is all conjecture, I will try not to condemn him. And besides, perhaps there was not much affection in the case."

"Perhaps not," he agreed. "At least I hope not on the part of the young woman. But if Bingley was not smitten, it would lessen my cousin's triumph considerably."

Elizabeth smiled, but she could not bring herself to

say more. She was too angry to speak.

When she and the Colonel returned to the Parsonage, she felt no better. Mr. Collins was fussing over their invitation to drink tea at Rosings Park. The prospect of having to sit in a room and be civil to the odious Mr. Darcy was more than Elizabeth could bear. She said she was unwell, and in truth, it was no lie for she had a headache brought on by her agitation.

Charlotte was concerned and offered to stay with her, but Mr. Collins disagreed. "Lady Catherine will be displeased by Miss Bennet's staying at home. She will be livid if you stay home as well."

Charlotte nodded and hurried to finish her preparations.

Elizabeth was relieved when they finally left. She was glad to be alone and hoped that reading some of Jane's recent letters would give her peace.

* * *

Darcy met with his cousin Colonel Fitzwilliam in the hallway outside his room. "Where did you escape to? I thought we were going to play a game of chess."

"I took my annual tour of the Park."

Darcy said, "I would have joined you, if you had asked."

The Colonel shrugged. "I was not lonely. By good

fortune I met Miss Bennet and we had a lively conversation."

How lively, Darcy wondered sourly but decided not to ask. Then later when the Collinses appeared at tea, he discovered that Elizabeth had remained at the parsonage. Mrs. Collins said that she had a headache.

Lady Catherine began a lecture about the proper preparation of tisanes for headaches, and Darcy excused himself, saying that he had some pressing business. But instead of going up to his bedroom, he left Rosings and walked over to the parsonage.

Every step brought him closer to Elizabeth, to the woman he loved. He knew he was acting rashly, that his family and friends would be appalled, but he could not live another day without declaring himself. He thought of her constantly and he feared that if he did not act quickly, his cousin might propose first. He would not want to live knowing that she belonged to another.

A servant led him to the sitting room. He found Elizabeth at a table, reading a letter which she quickly folded and placed in the pocket of her day dress. He had a jealous thought – could the letter be from Wickham? He enquired after her health and said he had come, hoping that she were better.

"I am well enough," she said coolly.

He sat down for a few moments, trying to compose his thoughts, then got up and walked about the room. He walked towards her and said, "In vain have I struggled. It will not do. My feelings will not be repressed. You must allow me to tell you how ardently I admire and love you."

* * *

Elizabeth could not believe what she was hearing. Mr. Darcy loved her? She stared at him, stunned and silent.

He continued. "I believe I have loved you since your visit to Netherfield. I was concerned at first because your position in life, your family and connections are beneath my own. I worried that by marrying you, I would disappoint my friends and family. I worried that you might not be able to be a proper mistress to Pemberley. And on a more serious note, I did not want some of your sisters' and your mother's behaviour to influence my own sister, Georgiana."

Elizabeth flinched. She knew her family was not ideal, but her mother and sisters were merely silly. They would not harm his sister.

"I told myself that my feelings for you were only infatuation, but as we grew to know each other better, my admiration and passion grew. By the Netherfield Ball, I was besotted.

"I had no idea."

"No, for I strove to mask my feelings. After the Ball, I fled to London, determined to put you behind me. But I could not forget you, in spite of all my efforts. I kept thinking of you, and then when I saw you again here at Rosings, I knew that nothing could extinguish love I feel.

He spoke clearly. "Miss Bennet, I hope now, after hearing my tale, you will take compassion upon me and reward me with the thing I most desire – your hand in matrimony."

Elizabeth's mind raced. She did not like Mr. Darcy or his manners. Did he think to win her hand by telling her how inferior she and her family were? Apart from that, she was still offended and furious that he had separated Mr. Bingley from Jane. But as Charlotte often reminded her, he was worth ten thousand pounds a year, likely more. She also remembered what Mr. Collins had said when he proposed, urging her to accept him. He had said it was unlikely she would ever receive another proposal.

That statement, although unkind, was true. What were her odds of receiving a third proposal?

Slim to none after her father died and their family circumstances were significantly reduced.

She saw the future before her: a lonely spinsterhood,

living with her unhappy mother.

If she did not marry Mr. Darcy, she feared that a few years from now, she would regret it bitterly.

"Miss Bennet," Mr. Darcy continued. "Please speak. I am waiting with apprehension and as you delay, my anxiety grows."

He spoke of anxiety, but his countenance expressed real security. She could tell he had no doubt of a favourable response.

Could she live the rest of her life with such an arrogant, conceited man?

But he was better than Mr. Collins, she thought. At least he was intelligent and she enjoyed sparring with him.

And if she married him, she might be able to bring Mr. Bingley and Jane back together.

"Yes," she said clearly. "I will marry you."

She felt somewhat like Julius Caesar crossing the Rubicon. The die was cast. There was no turning back.

She had never seen Mr. Darcy look so happy. For once he looked almost amiable, approachable. He caught her hands in his in a moment of passion. His eyes blazed at her. He brought her hands to his lips and kissed them, first the backs, then turning her hands over, each palm.

Good heavens, Elizabeth thought, shivering at his

touch. What is next?

Then he seemed to collect himself. He released her hands and stood straighter. "Thank you, Miss Bennet. Elizabeth," he amended in a more formal manner, yet using her Christian name. "You have made me the happiest of men."

At least one of them was happy. She felt a sick weight of dread growing in her chest.

He said, "I assume I will stay longer with my aunt and travel with you down to Longbourn."

How could he talk of plans so calmly? She said flatly, "If possible, I would prefer a special license rather than posting the banns. My father is in ill health and it is possible that he could die before the banns were complete."

"And you wouldn't wish to marry while in mourning. Yes, I see that." He frowned as he considered this information. "The Colonel and I will leave tomorrow as planned. I will go to London, get the license and return to Longbourn as soon as possible."

She watched as he thought out loud. He said, "But now, I must return to Rosings. They will have missed me and may wonder where I have been."

"Your aunt, I think, will not be happy to hear of our engagement."

"No, for she wants me to marry my cousin Anne. But rest assured, Elizabeth, Anne and I have never been engaged. We are more like brother and sister and have never wished to marry. And as for my aunt, I will inform her of the wedding after I have spoken to your father."

He spoke as if obtaining her father's permission was a matter of course. Did the thought never cross his mind that her father could refuse him? But she knew that he would not. He would be relieved that she had found a way to secure her future as well as provide for her family.

She said stiffly, "I believe that would be best."

He nodded. "Until then. Thank you again, dearest, loveliest Elizabeth."

His words were calm, but his eyes still burned as they looked at her.

When the door closed, Elizabeth sank down into a chair and covered her face with her hands.

What have I done?

Mr. Darcy and the Colonel left the next day as planned and Elizabeth finished her visit with the Collinses a week later. As she rode back to Longbourn with Maria Lucas, she could not help but think of her future.

Mrs. Darcy. She would be mistress of Pemberley.

She hoped she had made the right choice. Mr. Darcy said he loved her, so theoretically she would not have to change to please him. But then again, her parents had loved each other in the beginning, and they had grown apart. She would endeavour to make Mr. Darcy happy in the hopes that the marriage would be tolerable.

She smiled, remembering what he had said about her at the Meryton Assembly. She could say something similar about him now as a potential husband. *He is tolerable, I suppose, and rich enough to tempt me.*

If she could find humour in the situation, she would not be so worried. After all, how bad could marriage to Mr. Darcy be? She would learn like Charlotte Lucas to maximize the pleasant aspects of her life and minimize the unpleasant. Perhaps she would be able to spend the majority of her days in a sitting room, avoiding her husband.

When she returned home, her father was pleased to see her, but Elizabeth could not believe the change in him. He looked even more thin and pale, but to her surprise, no one in the household seemed to have noticed it. Mrs. Bennet thought he had a cold and told him to stay in the library. "I am sure you could use the rest and we would prefer not to hear your coughing."

"Anything to make you happy, my dear," he said

with a wry smile in Elizabeth's direction. "It is the least I can do."

Elizabeth spoke to her father privately in the library as soon as she could arrange it. He sat in a tall backed chair by the fireplace with a blanket over his lap and motioned for her to sit down as well. "So, Lizzy, you have returned and I am still alive."

"I am glad to see it," she said. "How do you feel?"

"Abominably," he said, then smiled weakly. "My abominable abdomen. That sounds like one of Mary's elocution exercises."

"Is there nothing that can be done?"

"Laudanum," he said flatly. "It is merely a matter of time."

"And you don't wish to tell our mother?"

"I don't want to hear her wailing. Let me die in peace, Lizzy."

She must respect his wishes. "Yes, sir." She said, "And for your information, I have accepted a proposal from Mr. Darcy. He will be here in a few days to ask your permission."

"Then I suppose I must live a few more weeks, eh, Lizzy?"

"Two or three, if you can manage it."

He smiled at her gallows humour. "I will see what I can do."

"Thank you."

He mused. "Mr. Darcy? I am impressed. He seemed the sort of man to never look at a woman but to see a blemish. I am surprised he even looked at you."

"Apparently he noticed me at Netherfield."

"Ah, your mother was right about the powers of dancing to bring a man to the sticking point."

Elizabeth nodded.

He sighed. "I had hoped for better for you, Lizzy. He is a proud, unpleasant sort of man."

"I hope he will improve upon further acquaintance."

"And now you sound more like Jane than yourself."

"Can you wish me well?" Elizabeth said. "I would like your blessing."

"Are you having second thoughts? Do you want me to refuse him when he comes calling?"

"No, I have made up my mind, that it is the best for all concerned."

Her father nodded. "I doubt any of them will appreciate the magnitude of your sacrifice. Your mother will only see the fine clothes and carriages you will have."

"Do you have any counsel?"

"Strive to appreciate your husband. Learn to respect him. Otherwise, your lively disposition may lead you to discredit and misery."

"I hope I am not so foolish."

Her father shook his head. "We are all foolish. It is merely a matter of degree. But enough of this. I am too tired to discuss it further. You have made your choice and I will respect it."

Elizabeth knew she could not expect for more. Her father, for all his flaws, was an honest man.

He added in a gentler tone, "I do wish you well and hope that your unequal marriage eventually prospers. Give me a kiss, Lizzy."

She reached down and kissed his cheek. "Thank you, Father."

She spent a few minutes collecting herself, then sought out Jane to speak to her privately as well.

"Oh, Elizabeth, this cannot be," her older sister said. "You must be joking. I know how much you dislike the man."

Elizabeth hesitated. Yes, she still disliked him, but she did not want to add to Jane's worries. For the first time, she held part of her heart back from her sister. She smiled. "I would hardly accept his proposal if I disliked him completely. In Hunsford I came to appreciate more of his good qualities."

Ten thousand good qualities.

Jane sighed, relieved. "Then I am glad, and I do

congratulate you. I have always thought he could not be as bad as Mr. Wickham painted." She smiled. "His manners can be a little stiff, but he is such a tall, handsome man."

"Yes," Elizabeth agreed.

"Well educated."

"Yes."

"And from all reports a good brother."

"Yes."

Jane said, "But are you quite certain that you can be happy with him? Sometimes when you conversed with him, I felt that you were more like combatants than lovers."

"That is our way," Elizabeth said lightly. "Not everyone wants to quote poetry and stare meaningfully into each other's eyes."

Jane laughed. "I suppose so. I just don't want you to marry without affection. Are you quite sure that you feel what you ought to do?"

Oh Jane, Elizabeth thought. Do not make me perjure myself. "There are a thousand different ways for men and women to fall in love and become married. Who is to say which way is best? Do you remember what you said when Charlotte accepted Mr. Collins? You told me to make allowances for differences of situation and temper. Well, given my situation and temper, I believe that Mr. Darcy is the ideal man for me."

"Then I am truly happy for you, Lizzy," Jane said and embraced her.

* * *

Within a few days of her return, Mrs. Bennet bustled with the news that Mr. Bingley was returning to Netherfield Park. "Oh, Jane," she said happily. "I see that his attraction to you cannot be denied. And Mr. Bennet, you must wait on him the moment he arrives."

"No," their father said. "If he wants our society, let him seek it. He knows where we live. I will not spend my hours in running after my neighbours every time they go away and come back again. Besides, I am too tired."

Mrs. Bennet tsked her tongue in irritation. "Mr. Bennet, I believe you are determined to vex me and my poor nerves."

Mr. Bennet said, "Your poor nerves will outlive us all," then he turned and smiled at Jane. "I hope Mr. Bingley's return is good news for you, Jane."

Jane shook her head. "Please, do not tease me, Father. Mr. Bingley should be able to return to the house he has rented without everyone building false hopes."

"False hopes are better than none. Don't you agree, Mary?"

Elizabeth's younger sister Mary considered herself something of a philosopher. "I believe it is best to keep one's feet firmly on the ground of reality and yet, still gaze upward into the sky of hope."

Lydia rolled her eyes at this homespun wisdom and announced, "Lizzy, I have some excellent news, capital news, about a certain person that we all like." Elizabeth turned toward her.

"I see your smile," Lydia added. "And I would make you guess, but you never will."

"If you'll excuse me," Mr. Bennet said. "I will leave you to your scintillating conversation."

Lydia waited until her father had left to announce, "Mary King's uncle has taken her off to Liverpool, gone to stay. Wickham is safe."

"They are no longer engaged?"

"No."

That meant Wickham could have married her, if he were so inclined and if she had not already agreed to marry Mr. Darcy. But that was foolishness. Her family could not live on a soldier's income. And she did not want to be any man's second choice. At least Mr. Darcy had professed to love her and did so, knowing that it could alienate his family.

Elizabeth felt a pang of remorse for marrying a man who loved her when she did not love him. It did not seem fair. But then, he had not required that of her. He had not bothered to ask. No doubt, it would never occur to him that she would not adore him. For years women like Miss Bingley had pursued him and he had grown conceited. He would never imagine that any young woman could find him lacking in any way.

Kitty said, "Miss King is a great fool for going away if she liked Wickham."

Jane said, "I hope there is no strong attachment on either side."

Lydia said, "I'm sure there is none on his. How could he care for such a nasty little freckled thing?"

Jane gasped. "Lydia, that is unkind."

Mrs. Bennet intervened. "I'm certain Mr. Wickham had his reasons for liking Miss King."

Ten thousand reasons, Elizabeth thought, and shuddered as her conscience condemned her. She was not certain she liked herself right now. How was she any better than Wickham?

"And she had hers for going to Liverpool," Mrs. Bennet continued. "A young woman with a fortune can choose to be particular. As much as Mr. Wickham is very handsome in his regimentals, she could probably do better. She might even be able to marry a Baronet."

"I don't think there's anyone better than Wickham," Lydia announced. "Don't you agree, Lizzy?"

Jane looked at Elizabeth, her eyes wide. Elizabeth knew she thought now would be a good time to mention Mr. Darcy, but until he arrived at Longbourn and spoke to her father, their upcoming wedding was not reality. So she merely smiled and Lydia rattled on. Lydia, like her mother, did not need active participants in her conversations.

CHAPTER THREE

Darcy was glad to return to Netherfield, but his younger sister Georgiana was a poor traveller. Riding in a carriage often gave her a headache, so she sat across from him with a frown on her face, saying little.

Charles, on the other hand, was excited about returning and renewing his acquaintance with the Bennet family and could not stop mentioning it.

Unfortunately, Charles had also brought along his sister Caroline, and in her conceit, she thought Darcy was attracted to her. She teased him, as she had before. "Are you also looking forward to spending time with the Bennets, Mr. Darcy?"

"Yes, that is part of my plan."

"I don't know why. They are such a tedious family. I agree that Jane Bennet is a pretty girl, but I never understood why Miss Eliza was considered a beauty. Her face is too thin; her complexion has no brilliancy;

and her features are not at all handsome. I remember your saying one night when they had been dining at Netherfield, 'She a beauty! – I should as soon call her mother a wit.'"

That had been ungracious, and Darcy regretted that he had given Miss Bingley ammunition to taunt him.

She added, "But afterwards she seemed to improve upon you."

"Yes, she has."

Miss Bingley could not let the subject die. "In what way?"

"I am no artist. I cannot define her features. But now I consider her one of the handsomest women of my acquaintance."

Georgiana's eyes widened at this remark and Miss Bingley stiffened. She was silent for a few minutes, then said archly, "I wonder how Mrs. Bennet will like Pemberley. I believe that once she comes, she will never leave."

Darcy frowned at that and Miss Bingley smirked. He would like to tell her about the engagement, but until it was official, he would keep his silence. In order to ignore Miss Bingley, he looked out the carriage window and thought about Elizabeth, instead.

How glad he would be when they had left Longbourn and were safely settled at Pemberley. He would enjoy giving her a tour of the house and lands, sharing his favourite rooms and locations. And once they were married, he would commission a portrait. He wanted to see her likeness hanging in the portrait gallery. And later, when they had children, he would commission more portraits. He imagined Elizabeth seated in a garden, surrounded by several children. He hoped that they would have more than two children. He had been the only child for ten years and had been pleased when Georgiana was born. But she had been a girl and the difference in their ages so great that she had never been a companion to him. And when he became her guardian, he had taken a parental role.

He had not realized until recently now how solitary his life had been. He had many acquaintances but few friends. Even Bingley, who was one of his closer friends, did not know all his thoughts.

He hoped that in marrying Elizabeth he had found a woman in whom he could confide. He hoped she could be what the Bible referred to as a helpmeet: a true companion.

Darcy and Bingley called on the Bennets the next day. Elizabeth was sitting with some embroidery in her lap. Her gaze met his when he entered the room. She blushed and looked away. He felt a surge of pride and possession. She was so beautiful. It made him happy to know that she had agreed to be his wife. He was glad he had a special license and would not have to wait long for the ceremony.

Mrs. Bennet was worse that he remembered: more loud and vulgar. He did not look forward to having her at Pemberley. She fawned over Bingley, greeting him with an excess of civility, whereas she was cold and ceremonious to him.

"It is a long time, Mr. Bingley since you went away," said Mrs. Bennet.

"Yes, ma'am."

"We thought you would return much sooner. I suppose you have heard that Charlotte Lucas married."

"Yes ma'am."

Darcy looked at Elizabeth, wondering if she would ever tell him of Mr. Collins' proposal. He would have to tell her how grateful he was that she had refused him.

"And Jane visited her aunt and uncle in London. It is a shame you never met."

Bingley spoke to Jane. "When were you in Town?"

"Earlier this year."

Bingley said, "I wish I had known."

Mrs. Bennet continued. "And Elizabeth went to visit the Collinses in March. She is just recently returned. I believe she met your aunt, Mr. Darcy, Lady

Catherine de Bourgh."

He looked at Elizabeth sharply. Had she told her family nothing of her visit? "Yes, I was there as well."

"Indeed," Mrs. Bennet said, apparently not interested. She turned back to Bingley. "Do you intent to stay in the country long, Mr. Bingley?"

"A few weeks," he said.

"Well, when you have killed all your own birds, Mr. Bingley. I beg you will come here, and shoot as many as you please, on Mr. Bennet's manor. I am sure he will be vastly happy to oblige you, and will save all the best covies for you."

Darcy watched as Bingley struggled to find the appropriate response to this excessive, officious attention. After a moment, Darcy said, "Excuse me, ma'am. I have brought a book for Mr. Bennet. May I speak with him privately?"

"Certainly, sir."

A servant escorted him to the library. "Mr. Darcy," he announced.

"Forgive me for not standing," Mr. Bennet said as Darcy entered the room. "Please close the door."

Darcy obliged.

"My daughter told you of my ill health and that I will die soon?"

"Yes, sir. I was sorry to hear it."

"Yes, well, there is nothing to be done about it now. Have a seat. From my daughter's conversation, you have something of import to tell me."

"Yes, I would like to marry your daughter and seek your permission to do so."

Mr. Bennet nodded. "Why Lizzy? You are a wealthy man with a fine estate. You could have your pick of almost any young woman in England. Why did you choose her?"

"Because I love her."

"Love can be fleeting. What is considered love is often no more than infatuation."

Darcy saw that his future father-in-law was concerned about whether he would be constant. "I have cared for your daughter for several months now. This is no infatuation."

"And what do you value most about her?"

"It is difficult to say. She is beautiful and clever. There is a lightness and a joy in her nature. But underneath that, she has integrity and she is loyal." He thought of the way she championed Wickham. He did not like that, but it showed she had a generous and brave heart. She was also a good friend to Mrs. Collins and a faithful sister to Jane.

"Yes, she is loyal. She would make any sacrifice for those she loves."

Mr. Bennet's voice trailed off as if he was lost in his own thoughts. Darcy waited, then after a minute said, "Do I have your blessing?"

"Yes, indeed, on one condition."

Darcy steeled himself, wondering what financial demands Mr. Bennet would make.

"Be kind to her."

He stiffened at the suggestion that he would be otherwise. "I have no intension of being unkind."

"None of us do," Mr. Bennet said. "But it is easy to let little inconveniences and miscommunications vex us, to cause a rift between those who should take the highest care for each other."

Mr. Bennet sounded as if he spoke from experience.

"I will care for her every need," Darcy promised. "You have not asked of it, but I have brought letter outlining the settlement I am prepared to make on her behalf."

Mr. Bennet waved his hand. "I know you are wealthy, Mr. Darcy. That is not my concern. My daughter is a jewel, a rare and beautiful gem. You've seen her sisters – none, not even Jane, can compare to her. She deserves a man who will treasure her."

"I will treasure her."

"That remains to be seen, and I will not live to know whether you do or not. So, as one man to another I am asking you to be kind."

Darcy thought of his own father and the promises he had made to him on his deathbed. Promises to care for Georgiana and to keep Pemberley free of debt. He imagined that one day he would ask his own son for promises as well. As if the prior generation could have any control over the future. But one must try, nevertheless. "I will," he said. The words were like a vow.

* * *

When Darcy returned from speaking to her father, he returned to the sitting room. He caught Elizabeth's eye and nodded.

It was done, Elizabeth thought. Her father had given his permission, and now she must tell her mother, but she did not want to do it when Mr. Darcy was present. She did not know whether her mother would be appalled or pleased, but whatever her response, it would not be moderate, and she wanted to spare her future husband the dramatics. "I will tell my mother later today," she whispered to him when she had the chance.

"And I will make arrangements with the rector."

"Thank you."

Mr. Bingley rose to end the visit and invited

everyone to come to tea at Netherfield that afternoon. "My sister and Miss Georgiana would enjoy the company."

"Oh, Jane, what a delight," Mrs. Bennet said after the gentlemen had left. "You must all go. I will arrange with your father for the carriage. It is too bad you must endure Mr. Darcy too, but perhaps his sister will be nice."

Elizabeth blushed, embarrassed for her mother. "Mama," she said. "May I speak with you alone for a few minutes?"

"Yes, if you must," Mrs. Bennet said. "You are not ill, are you?"

"No, not at all."

"Very well. Mary, Jane, please leave us." Kitty and Lydia had gone to Meryton so they were not present.

Elizabeth waited until her sisters had left, then said, "Mama, I am engaged to be married."

"Do not tease me, child."

"No, I am serious. Mr. Darcy has proposed, I have accepted, and Father has given his blessing."

"Mr. Darcy?" Mrs. Bennet gasped and for nearly a full minute, she was silent, unable to utter a syllable. When she began to recover, she said, "Dear me. Good gracious. Mr. Darcy? He is so tall! Are you absolutely certain?"

Elizabeth assured her that she was.

"Oh my. Sweetest Lizzy!" she said and embraced her. "You have saved us all. How rich and great you will be! What pin money! I am so pleased – so happy."

She then coloured. "I do hope he doesn't realize how much I've disliked him. I hope he will overlook it."

Elizabeth hoped so as well.

"How soon can you be married?" she asked.

"He has obtained a special license."

"Excellent. I do hope your father has recovered by then. Mr. Bennet doesn't like to admit it, but his cold has brought him very low. I think perhaps I should talk to Mr. Jones and see what he can do. Perhaps a fortifying draught."

Elizabeth bit her lip. "That might be best."

"I shall send a note to fetch him." She sighed. "Mr. Darcy. I still cannot believe it. Ten thousand a year, and very likely more. Tis as good as a Lord. Oh Lizzy, you are so clever. I never thought you had it in you."

Elizabeth did not want to continue that line of thought. "If you will excuse me, ma'am, I should get ready to visit Netherfield."

"Oh yes, indeed," her mother said. "And wear your prettiest gown. And let Sarah prepare your hair. We don't want Mr. Darcy to change his mind."

* * *

At Netherfield, Darcy introduced Elizabeth to his sister Georgiana. She was a lovely young woman, tall and graceful. Elizabeth could see the family resemblance with her dark hair and eyes. "It is a p-pleasure to m-meet you M-miss Bennet," Miss Darcy said.

Elizabeth was surprised by the stammer. "The pleasure is mine, Miss Darcy."

Miss Darcy smiled and nodded, but did not say anything else. Elizabeth assumed that it must be difficult to converse with a stammer and her heart went out to the girl.

Miss Bingley served the tea. She sat by Jane and said how nice it was to see her again and asked if she had enjoyed her visit to London.

Bingley looked surprised. "You knew?"

Miss Bingley said, "I'm certain I told you, brother. I visited Miss Bennet at her uncle's home in Cheapside."

Bingley said, "If I had known, Miss Bennet, I would have called as well."

Elizabeth thought that Darcy looked a little uncomfortable at this speech and she wondered what he was thinking, but said nothing. She knew he would not want to call in Cheapside, which was a shame because her Aunt and Uncle Gardiner were the most respectable of her relations. She did not know whether they would be able to come to the wedding.

Miss Bingley changed the subject. "Miss Eliza, I have heard a rumour that the militia are planning to leave Meryton. Is that true?"

"I believe so." Indeed, Lydia and Kitty had talked of little else since she had returned home. Lydia was hoping to travel to Brighton with the Colonel's wife, but Mr. Bennet had yet to give his approval. Elizabeth knew he was concerned that depending upon the time of his death, there could be additional travel costs to bring her back.

"That will be a great loss to your family."

Elizabeth knew that she was referencing Wickham and was relieved she did not mention him by name in front of Darcy. She did not want to stir up trouble. "We shall survive," Elizabeth said wryly.

Georgiana stood. "Forgive m-me, please excuse me. I would like to lie d-down," she said. "I h-have a h-headache."

Immediately Darcy was at her side. He escorted her from the room and returned a few minutes later.

"Poor Miss Darcy," Miss Bingley crooned. "There is nothing worse than a headache. I hope the rest does her well. Do you think she will be able to join us later for dinner?"

"I do not know," Darcy said coolly, then spoke to Elizabeth abruptly. "Miss Elizabeth, would you care for a walk in the garden?"

"By yourselves?" Miss Bingley teased. "Do you have secret affairs to discuss?"

Darcy drew himself up to his full height. "Actually, yes, but there is no point in keeping all of them private now. Miss Bennet and I are engaged to be married and I wish to discuss some of the particulars with her. If you will excuse us."

Elizabeth watched the reaction of the other people in the room. It was almost as entertaining as a play. Jane was pleased. Mr. Bingley was surprised. "Congratulations, Darcy. This is capital news."

Miss Bingley's mouth gaped open in astonishment, but then her eyes flashed. "If this is a joke, it is in poor taste. Don't let him bandy your reputation, Miss Eliza."

"I am deadly serious," Mr. Darcy said.

"But how? Why?"

Mr. Darcy smiled coolly. "I think I first considered it after your suggestions. You made such a point of describing Miss Bennet's family as my future relations, that it gave me ideas."

At this, Miss Bingley blanched.

"Come, Elizabeth," he said, offering his hand. He

led her from the room, out double doors to the garden.

"Is that true?" she asked once they were alone. "Did you ask me to marry you because of Miss Bingley?"

"No," he said. "I began thinking of it much sooner than that, but I was tired of her teasings and wanted to shut her up."

"Remind me not to anger you," Elizabeth said.

"You think I was too harsh with her?"

"No, but I would hate to have you speak to me in that same tone."

Darcy smiled. "You need not fear. I love you." He punctuated the words by kissing her hand.

Elizabeth felt a blush rise in her cheek. She gently pulled her hand from his and he did not protest. She said, "It is a lovely day for a walk. Was there anything in particular you wished to discuss?"

He said, "Yes, I would like to talk to you about Georgiana."

"Is she not well?"

"No, she will be fine. She does not travel well, but the true source of her discomfort was Miss Bingley's mentioning the militia." He let his breath out slowly. "Normally I would not discuss the matter, but since you are to be my wife, I must. Last summer George Wickham tried to elope with Georgiana."

"But she is so young!"

"Yes, and he sought to take advantage of that."

Elizabeth knew there was no love lost between the two men, and this must be part of the reason. "Did they care for each other?"

"She thought herself in love. He only wanted her dowry, which is thirty thousand pounds."

It appeared Mr. Wickham had a habit of liking wealthy women. She never had a chance with him.

Darcy continued. "From prior conversations, I know you have thought well of him. I am not one to blithely divulge my family history, but in this case, I feel that I should. You know that Mr. Wickham was the son of my late father's steward."

"Yes, he told me."

"And my father liked him. He supported him in school and left him a living in his will."

"Which you denied."

"Which Wickham turned down in exchange for three thousand pounds."

She was surprised. "So much?"

"Yes. He did not wish to become a clergyman. He said he was going to study the law, but nothing came of that. I believe he wasted the entirety of the funds. When the living came vacant, two years ago, he returned, wanting me to give it to him. I refused and he left, angry and threatening."

This was all new information to Elizabeth. Part of her wanted to disbelieve it, but Darcy presented the facts so logically and calmly, she had to consider it. "This means that Wickham is not what he appears."

"No. I did not refuse the living merely for financial reasons. I refused because I knew he should not be a clergyman. He appears to be a man of honour, but he is not. He is selfish, immoral, profligate. I do not want to sully your ears with the details of his exploits, but trust me, if he had married my sister, her life would have been a misery. He has been the ruin of many other women before her. I don't know why they are drawn to him."

Elizabeth thought back, remembering Wickham's smiles, his charm. Was there nothing of substance to him? She tried to remember something, anything he had done to show his real character, and yet she could recall nothing more than his countenance, voice and manner. He had appeared to be good, so she had believed him. At least with Mr. Darcy, she knew he was a good friend to Bingley and a good brother. She asked, "And your sister?"

"Last summer she was in Ramsgate with a Mrs. Younge. I did not know at the time that Mrs. Younge knew Wickham. She was most likely one of his previous mistresses. In the end, she persuaded

Georgiana to meet with Wickham. He flattered her and convinced her that she was in love with him."

Elizabeth flushed. He had flattered her as well, and although she hadn't fallen in love with him, she might have. She was absolutely ashamed of herself. For years she had prided herself on her discernment and yet, she had been deceived by a handsome face and sugared words.

She felt as foolish as Kitty or Lydia.

Darcy continued. "Fortunately, I arrived for a visit the day before their planned elopement. Georgiana could not keep their secret and told me everything. You may imagine what I felt and how I acted."

"I am surprised Wickham is still living."

"Believe me, I would have gladly challenged him to a duel, but I did not want to endanger Georgiana's reputation. You and Colonel Fitzwilliam are the only ones who know of the matter."

Elizabeth said, "I will not tell anyone."

"I trust that. I merely thought you should know, so you can be a better sister to Georgiana."

"Was she terribly hurt?"

"Yes. She cried for days. I hoped that a London Season would restore her to happiness, but she says she will not go. She is too self-conscious."

"Of her stammer?"

"Yes. It is worse when she is nervous or unhappy. At other times it is hardly noticeable."

Elizabeth thought perhaps that he was speaking from brotherly kindness rather than actuality. "Is there anything that can be done?"

Darcy shook his head. "We've seen numerous doctors, trying different diets and speech exercises, but so far, none of them have helped."

"That is a shame. She seems to be a lovely girl."

"She is, and I hope one day she will find a man who loves her for herself and not merely for her fortune."

At that moment, Elizabeth hesitated. She knew that Darcy deserved that as well as his sister, but it was too late to back out now.

Could she grow to care for him? Today, having learned the truth about Wickham, made her rethink everything. Mr. Darcy might still be an arrogant man, but he had a good reason for being harsh with Wickham. And no doubt he thought he had a good reason for separating Jane and Bingley as well.

As for her sister and his friend, she would endeavour to change Darcy's mind.

CHAPTER FOUR

Mrs. Bennet's nerves seemed to increase as the day of Elizabeth's wedding drew closer. She worried that something would ruin the day, and true to her fears, Mr. Bennet was not ready when it was time to leave for the church. "It does not matter if your father is late to every other social obligation, but a man should not be late to his daughter's wedding," she said irritably. "What if Mr. Darcy is offended? Girls, go wait in the carriage. Lizzy, would you please fetch your father?"

Elizabeth dutifully knocked on the library door. "Father, may I come in?"

There was no answer, so she knocked a second time and then opened the door. She found her father lying on a couch, eyes closed.

Fear gripped her heart but as she approached, she saw that he was still breathing, although his breath was shallow. "Father?" she said. "What is wrong?"

JANE GRIX

"I was ill," he said weakly and pointed to a bowl by the fireplace. "And I laid down to rest. I stained my waistcoat. I am sorry if I am inconveniencing the family."

"No, that is fine," Elizabeth said, relieved that he could still speak. "Do you need help with walking?"

"Yes," he said. "Fetch John and I will lean on him."

"Yes, sir."

John came, assisted with a change of waistcoat and helped him into the entryway.

Mrs. Bennet looked at him with a critical eye, noting his dishevelled hair and pale skin. "Good heavens, Mr. Bennet. Have you imbibed the celebratory wine early? Are you foxed?"

"No, ma'am, I am dying."

Mrs. Bennet seemed not to hear him for a moment, but as his words made more sense, she shrieked and fainted.

Mr. Bennet turned to Elizabeth. "I am sorry, Lizzy. I am spoiling your wedding day after all."

Hill brought the smelling salts and Jane waived them under her mother's nose. Eventually Mrs. Bennet roused. "Oh Mr. Bennet," she wailed. "Why did you not tell me? How bad is it? What do the doctors say? Is there no hope?"

Mr. Bennet said, "We can discuss this later, after

the wedding breakfast."

"Oh yes, the wedding," Mrs. Bennet said frantically. "Thank goodness for Mr. Darcy. And we must hurry. We don't want him to have to wait."

Elizabeth reached for Jane's hand and squeezed it. "Is it very bad?" Jane asked.

Elizabeth nodded.

"How long have you known?"

Elizabeth shrugged. "A few weeks now."

Jane looked troubled. "And you could not tell me?"

"Father did not want me to."

* * *

Darcy dressed early and rode early to the church. The ceremony could not happen soon enough for him. He hoped the breakfast at Longbourn would not last long and that he and Elizabeth would soon be on the road.

He paced back and forth, waiting for Elizabeth to appear. Georgiana teased him that he was like a lion in the London zoo.

Her comments made him check himself. He did not want to appear ridiculous, so he stood still, waiting for his bride.

Finally she appeared. Her father looked ill and her mother was red faced and red eyed as if she had been crying. Fortunately, Elizabeth smiled and nodded as if to tell him that everything would be fine.

Within minutes the rector started the familiar words of the ceremony. Darcy watched Elizabeth. She looked down, as if shy, which surprised him. She was normally so lively and quick, his heart was touched to think that she could be nervous. Darcy felt a surge of love and affection for her. She was so lovely. He spoke his vows with conviction. "With this ring, I thee wed, with my Body I thee worship, and with all my worldly Goods I thee endow."

Her hand trembled in his.

Once outside, they kissed briefly. Too briefly for him, but he was not one to display his affections before a crowd.

At the Longbourn breakfast, Mrs. Bennet cornered him. "Oh, Mr. Darcy. Have you heard the news about my poor husband?"

"Yes, ma'am. It is a great sorrow."

Mrs. Bennet nodded and dabbed her face with a crumpled handkerchief. "I don't know what we will do if you don't take care of us, Mr. Darcy."

"I will be happy to help."

He glanced at Elizabeth who looked at him with gratitude.

"Mr. Collins will throw us out into the streets before Mr. Bennet is even cold in his grave."

"You will not be homeless, ma'am." He would not have them all at Pemberley, but he would arrange a rental property. Hopefully in Hertfordshire, rather than Derbyshire, but he would deal with that problem when it arose.

Mrs. Bennet patted his arm. "Oh Mr. Darcy, you are too good to us."

Darcy was glad when the press of other well-wishers separated them. He accepted the congratulations from Elizabeth's various family and neighbours. He spoke briefly to Bingley, who had been conversing with Jane Bennet.

At one point, he could not find Elizabeth and Jane said she had gone upstairs to get something from her room. Darcy left the crowd to look for her. As he passed the hallway, he saw two of his sister-in-laws whispering and giggling together. He started up the stairs and overheard Lydia say clearly, "I pity Lizzy. I don't know how she could marry him, considering how she feels. I don't care how rich Mr. Darcy is. I would never marry a man I hated."

The words stunned him. Darcy told himself that it was just the youngest Bennet girl being silly, but when he went upstairs to Elizabeth's room, he saw her sitting on her bed, looking out the window with a pensive expression, and he wondered if it could be true.

She couldn't hate him. She would not have married him if she hated him. Or would she? How well did he know her? For the first time, he realized that in all their conversations, she had never expressed her love for him.

And once she had agreed to marry him, she had not teased him. Whenever she spoke to him, her conversation had been brisk, matter-of-fact. Had the clever banter been her way to secure his affection?

Had he been duped?

Had she merely been more proficient in her wiles than Miss Bingley?

He said, "Elizabeth, are you all right?"

She startled, then smiled. "Did you miss me?" she asked archly. "Do not worry, I will be downstairs shortly."

There was no amusement in her eyes. She was dismissing him. She did not want to speak to him. He began to feel as if he was in a nightmare.

He said stiffly, "I would like to leave within a half hour."

She nodded. "I will be ready. I merely wish to say farewell to my bedroom."

He looked at her more closely. "Are you crying?"

"A little." She brought a handkerchief to her eyes. "I am thinking about my father. I doubt I will see him again."

Darcy realized that he had been oblivious. Naturally, Elizabeth was sorrowful. There was a reason she did not tease him. Her father was dying. Even if she was happy to marry him, she could not ignore that reality and it was casting a pall over her good humour. He set aside his doubts. "Forgive me. You will miss your family."

"But now I have a new family with you." She held out her hand and he took it gratefully. He sat beside her on the bed. Now that they were man and wife it was no impropriety.

He said gently, "It is not a fair trade. You have given me six new family members, whereas I have only given you Georgiana."

She smiled, amused. "Neither of us will comment on the quality rather than quantity of that exchange. I know you do not like my mother and my sisters irritate you."

This was the Elizabeth he knew, teasing and challenging him. He relaxed and said, "Not all of them. I quite like Jane."

She gave a little laugh. "How magnanimous, Mr. Darcy. How could anyone not like Jane? She could never irritate anyone. She is too good. Like your Mr. Bingley."

"Even Bingley irritates me, sometimes," he admitted.

Elizabeth nodded. "I agree. He irritates me as well. Not as much lately, however."

He looked at her inquisitively and she added, "I like him better now that he has returned to Netherfield."

"Why?"

Elizabeth hesitated, then said, "He appears to favour my sister, so I am inclined to like him better. But I fear he may be fickle, easily changing his affections with his location. A matter of 'out of sight, out of mind?' You know him best. Should I warn my sister?"

"Warn her, why?"

"To guard her heart, naturally."

Darcy was surprised. "She cares for him?"

Elizabeth seemed surprised as well. "Can there be any doubt?"

Darcy said, "Your sister has such a serene countenance and air. I knew she did not mind his attentions, but I had no idea that she encouraged them. I thought she was completely indifferent. She smiles at him as if he is an exuberant puppy, nothing more."

"Good heavens. Is that what you really thought?"

"That is what I have thought until now, but apparently I was in error. Your superior knowledge of your sister's affection must correct me. Does she love him?"

"My sister is reserved, but beneath that, her feelings run strong and true."

"Like you?" Darcy asked. He touched her cheek with a gentle caress.

Elizabeth gasped, but did not pull away. Her eyes widened.

How sweet, he thought and leaned forward to kiss her, but she put her fingers to his lips to check him. "I warn you, sir," she said. "I am no Jane. I am not as good or kind. I have a temper."

"So do I," he said, kissing her fingers. "But you bring out the best in me."

Someone giggled and then said, "Pardon me, Lizzy, Mr. Darcy. But Mama was asking for you."

Elizabeth's face flushed red and Darcy rose quickly to his feet, angry that the moment had been interrupted, embarrassed that his words had been overheard by – he looked at his sister-in-law – Kitty. He was appalled to think that their tender words would be gossip fodder in Meryton. "We will be down directly," he said coolly.

* * *

Elizabeth spoke one last time to Jane and gave her a hug. Jane whispered. "Be happy, Lizzy."

"I will do my best," Elizabeth promised. She had

been fearful at the wedding, overly concerned about the seriousness of the vows, but her conversation with Mr. Darcy upstairs had given her hope. When he had kissed her fingers, she had felt comfortable with him rather than apprehensive. Perhaps they could be happy together.

She reminded herself that many people married for fortune rather than affection, and that affection could grow over time.

Hugging her father one last time made her tears well up again. Mrs. Bennet was too overcome by emotion to do anything more than cry and wave her handkerchief. Kitty and Lydia giggled. Mary quoted Fordyce about the sanctity of marriage. Amidst the noise and confusion, she saw that Mr. Darcy spoke briefly to Mr. Bingley. Mr. Bingley looked astonished and then glanced at Jane who smiled and blushed.

Elizabeth smiled at her new husband. Marrying him was right if it meant that Jane could marry Bingley. She could almost forgive Mr. Darcy for his earlier interference if he was making amends now. He had misjudged Jane, but it was easy to understand why. She remembered what Charlotte had said months before – that Jane was too circumspect and that she should express her feelings more freely.

Elizabeth felt that the opposite was true for her. She

showed her feelings too clearly and needed to rein them in if she was to have a happy marriage. I will be more like Jane, she told herself.

Finally they were in the carriage, on the way to Darcy House in London. Miss Darcy and her companion Mrs. Annesley were going to stay at Netherfield Park for two weeks and then join them at Pemberley.

Elizabeth sat across from her silent husband, trying to think of something to say. Finally she said, "I thought the ceremony went well."

"Yes. And we were fortunate in the weather."

She sighed. This was not a promising beginning if they were reduced to discussing the weather within five minutes of being alone together. "My mother was worried about the cake. Did you like it?"

Darcy smiled. "Honestly? I do not remember. I care little for sweets."

Elizabeth filed this information away in her mind. Her new husband did not like sweets. They were both silent for several minutes. Elizabeth said, "I wish I could have met your parents."

"I wish that as well. They would have liked you."

Elizabeth was not sure of that. She remembered what he had said when he proposed. She wondered if his parents would have been appalled by his choice. "How long have they been gone?"

"My mother has been dead for nearly eight years. My father for the past five."

"You were young then, to inherit Pemberley."

"I was only twenty-three, but my father had prepared me. And I had an excellent steward. Which is not to say that the transfer of authority was easy. Or that I did not make mistakes."

"That does not sound like you. I thought you did not make mistakes."

"No, of course not," he said dryly. "I must have misspoken."

"Which would of itself be a mistake."

"True. You have tied me in knots now. I dare not speak at all."

Elizabeth gave a little laugh. "Which should be no hardship for you. Sometimes I think you make an effort to speak as little as possible."

"Sometimes," he agreed. "I have never been a great conversationalist in crowds. I don't have the talent which some people possess of conversing easily with those I have never seen before. I much prefer smaller gatherings. And in you, I have found one person I actually look forward to conversing with."

Elizabeth smiled at this gallantry. She had never considered the possibility that Mr. Darcy could be awkward around strangers. Perhaps she had misjudged him in this matter as well.

After another half hour of silence, she said, "I saw that you spoke to Bingley as we were leaving."

"Yes, I told him that I had changed my mind about your sister and that I now thought she liked him."

"Thank you for that. Now the matter is in his hands whether he will act on the information."

"I believe he will. I have never seen a man so besotted." Mr. Darcy gave a wry smile. "Except perhaps for myself."

She was reminded of his proposal. No doubt he thought he was besotted, but he still approached the matter methodically. And for all his talk of love, he stayed on the other side of the carriage, facing her. But then, he was a reserved man who would not want to make a spectacle of himself or give rise to gossip by becoming dishevelled in a carriage. She doubted he would kiss her before that evening.

She said, "Well, I hope Bingley proposes before my father dies." Once her family was in mourning, society would frown on any marriages performed before six months had passed. But then again, if Bingley was willing to wait that long, it would prove the depth of his affections for her sister.

She wondered if Mr. Darcy would have waited six months for her.

* * *

Darcy was pleased. Their first dinner at Darcy House was superb: the linens spotless, the silver gleaming, the several courses all hot and tasteful. Everything was going as he had planned. He looked across the table at Elizabeth. She was so beautiful. She was wearing the red dress that she had worn at Rosings. He thought she might be tired after their journey, so he had recommended that she rest before dinner. A new lady's maid had arranged her hair in an ornate style. It was lovely, but he was looking forward to seeing her hair down.

He planned for them to stay several days at Darcy House before going to Pemberley. He knew many people took elaborate wedding journeys, but he did not want to consummate his marriage in a strange bed in a new environment that he could not control. He did not want Elizabeth to have to deal with potentially poor food or service. He wanted to cherish her, and thought that would be best accomplished in his own home, with his own servants.

He thought they could take another journey, perhaps touring the Lake District later in the year.

He sat across from her at the table, both of them silent.

Occasionally Elizabeth caught his eye and then

looked down at her plate. Perhaps she was nervous about the evening to come. He was slightly nervous himself. He knew that as a gently bred young woman, she would come to their bed entirely inexperienced and he wanted her introduction to her marital duties to be as comfortable as possible. He remembered the advice his father had given him years before he came of age. "When you do marry, Fitzwilliam, remember to be considerate of your wife. A truly elegant young woman is not going to enjoy the physical aspects of marriage. She will endure it out of kindness and affection for you and for the hope of having children, but you must not take advantage of her good nature. Restrain yourself, and if necessary, acquire a mistress."

"Don't some women enjoy the process?" he had asked.

"I assume some of the lower classes," his father had said, visibly uncomfortable with the conversation. "And naturally, harlots will pretend. But whatever you do, be discreet. If you must go to a brothel, choose a better one and keep yourself clean."

"Yes, sir." At that point, he had been as embarrassed as his father.

They had never discussed the matter again.

After dinner Darcy wished that they could go directly to bed, but thought she would find his urgency crass. Instead he asked Elizabeth if she would play a song on the pianoforte. She played a piece by Handel, followed by a Scottish air. She was not as skilled as Georgiana, but she seemed to enjoy the process more, smiling as she played. Georgiana was more serious and often played with a look of intense concentration.

The clock on the mantle struck ten. Darcy asked her, "Would you like to retire?"

Elizabeth nodded. "Yes."

He offered her his arm and walked with her upstairs to their bedrooms that were connected by a door. Elizabeth was met by her new lady's maid. He said, "Good night. I will see you later."

* * *

Elizabeth took a deep breath after Darcy closed the door. I can do this, she thought. Mr. Darcy was a civilized man and since their marriage, he seemed determined to treat her with consideration and respect: asking her what she preferred, waiting for her, making certain she had a blanket for her lap in the carriage. He had arranged for a lady's maid by the name of Fisk, but had also told her that she could interview and find a replacement if she preferred.

Fisk helped her out of her evening dress. She was an older woman, possibly thirty, and seemed to know what she was doing. It was a new experience for Elizabeth to have a lady's maid all to herself. At home she had to share with her sisters and they often helped each other dress or undress. She mentally corrected herself. At Longbourn – not home. Her home was with Mr. Darcy now. Here at Darcy House and then at Pemberley.

Earlier that day Mr. Darcy had given her a ruby necklace that had been his mother's. The stones gleamed in the candlelight, dark red against her pale skin. Elizabeth had never owned a necklace so costly.

She unlatched the necklace and then placed it carefully in a locked jewellery box.

Fisk helped her with her hair. Without the pins and ribbons, her hair fell down her back. Elizabeth sat still while the maid brushed her hair. "I usually braid it," she said. "It is so curly and unruly."

"It is lovely, ma'am. Do you wish to keep it loose tonight?"

From her tone of voice, Elizabeth guessed that Fisk thought that would be best. Perhaps she thought Darcy would prefer her hair down. "No, I will have a braid." The maid obeyed without comment.

Back at Longbourn, Elizabeth slept in a high necked heavy cotton gown, but for tonight she had a thin gown, more sheer than she was accustomed to.

She put an embroidered morning robe over it and tied the ribbons that fastened beneath her breasts.

Fisk pulled down the sheets and made sure the fire was properly supplied. She also showed Elizabeth a small cupboard beside the bed that had a pitcher of water and soft towels. "For afterwards," she said quietly.

Elizabeth's face flamed. "How convenient," she said quietly. She wished she knew the woman well enough so she could ask her for advice – or that she had been able to speak to her Aunt Gardiner. Mrs. Gardiner seemed to be happier in her marriage than her mother, so she might have given better advice, but her health had not allowed her to travel to Longbourn.

Fisk said, "Will that be all?"

"Yes, thank you."

The maid left and closed the door behind her.

Darcy knocked on the connecting door, as if he had been waiting for the maid to leave. That was polite of him, Elizabeth thought. She supposed that some men would walk straight in, without asking.

"Come in," she said quietly.

When he came into the room, she saw that he was wearing a fine white night shirt open at the neck and a dark silk robe. His legs were bare. She could not look him in the eye and stared instead at his bare throat. She smiled. "I have never seen you without a cravat."

"And I have never seen you with your hair down," he said. "Although I have imagined it."

He sat beside her on the bed and touched the braid. "May I?" he asked, reaching for the ribbon at the end.

Apparently Fisk was right, Elizabeth thought. She sat patiently while he undid her hair. He was careful and thorough, releasing her hair without making it tangle. "It is so beautiful," he murmured. She looked at him, and he added, "You are so beautiful."

Elizabeth blushed. He sounded as if he adored her.

He reached over and kissed her. This kiss was like the one outside the church, but instead of pulling back, he leaned forward. He slid his fingers into her hair, cradling her head to bring her closer. He kissed her a second and third time. Elizabeth relaxed. He was persuasive rather than forceful, his hands gentle. Her breath quickened and she caught his shoulders to steady herself. He pulled back and his eyes were dark as they met hers. "I love you, Elizabeth."

She flinched.

"Is something wrong?" he asked.

She shook her head. "No," she said and made herself smile. She could not lie and tell him she loved him, but she must say something. She pushed aside a lock of his hair that had fallen on his forehead. "You have made me very happy today."

His eyes narrowed.

She sensed his uncertainty and leaned forward to kiss him, but he stiffened. "Elizabeth," he said coolly. "I am sorry, but there is something I need to ask you."

Elizabeth felt a moment of dread. His tone of voice reminded her of the Old Darcy, back when they were at Netherfield. She lifted her chin. "Yes?"

"I heard something today that your sister Lydia said."

"I'm sorry if she was rude or offended you, but you know how young and flighty she is."

"No, it was something I overheard. She did not speak to me directly."

"Perhaps you misheard her."

"Perhaps, I did. But I still would like to discuss it with you."

Elizabeth waited.

"Your sister said that you hate me."

"I don't hate you," she said quickly and wished for once that Lydia had been more circumspect. Why could she not guard her tongue?

"Then your sister's statement was groundless?"

Elizabeth's conscience struck her. It was not all Lydia's fault. "I may have said that before, but that was only when I first knew you."

Darcy frowned. "You hated me? Why?"

It sounded so foolish now. Elizabeth was embarrassed and appalled by her initial reaction to him. "It started at the Meryton Assembly. You said I was not handsome enough to tempt you."

Darcy drew his breath in sharply. "I did not mean for you to hear that."

"I did."

"And it wasn't true," he said. "I found you very tempting, which was why I did not want to dance with you. I apologize. I am sorry I was unkind at our first meeting, but it surprises me that you would react so strongly. Surely our later conversations showed you a better side of me."

This was going to be awkward. There was no way to say it nicely. "Not at first," Elizabeth said. "Your manners are formal, reserved. I thought you were arrogant. It was clear you looked down on most of the inhabitants of Meryton and found yourself superior. I was offended. And then when I learned you had harmed Mr. Wickham, I thought I hated you and I may have said that where Lydia could overhear. But I later learned that Mr. Wickham had lied and that you were not as bad as he had painted."

"But that was after we were engaged."

"Yes." It was difficult to remember now that she

had ever liked Wickham.

Darcy was quiet for a long moment. "Then you agreed to marry me, thinking me a villain."

If her husband ever chose to become a barrister, he would be excellent. She could imagine him confronting witnesses on the stand. She said, "Not exactly."

"Elizabeth. We are about to start our marriage and I think we should be completely honest with each other." He took her hands in his. "I want to know where I stand. I have told you of my love for you, but until today, I never questioned your feelings for me. I assumed that your feelings mirrored mine."

Her heart beat rapidly in her breast. She knew she had deceived him by letting him think she cared for him. If it was a lie, it had been a lie created by silence when she could have spoken. She chose her words cautiously. "My feelings may not be as strong as yours, but I do admire you, and I hope that we will be happy together." That at least was true.

"What exactly do you admire about me?"

"You are a good friend to Mr. Bingley. You care for your sister. You are a man of intelligence." Listed out loud, it did not sound like sufficient grounds for matrimony.

He nodded thoughtfully, his brow furrowed.

"I mean to be a good wife," she said desperately. *Please believe me.*

"And I appreciate that, but I am trying to understand your motivation. As much as I hate to say it, it appears that you married me for my fortune."

Elizabeth flushed. She could not answer him.

For a long moment the silence grew between them. She knew her mother and Charlotte would tell her to lie. But she could not lie, she respected him too much for that, and yet, she could not say the truth out loud, either. She could not condemn herself and make him think so poorly of her.

He appeared to experience a change of feeling. His expression which had been so amiable and open became harder. He straightened his shoulders. "Well, Mrs. Darcy," he said finally, his words clipped. "We understand each other now. I should have realized the truth sooner. As a man of fortune, I have often been sought for my wealth. Congratulations. You have made your mother proud."

Elizabeth supposed she deserved that. She had wounded his pride.

He continued, "I beg your pardon for my excess of adoration. I hope you did not find my attentions distasteful or uncomfortable."

"No. I did not." Could he not tell? She found his

kisses pleasant, much better than she had anticipated.

"Looking back, I realize that you never encouraged my advances, you merely endured them."

"Endure is too harsh a word."

"Tell me, since you do not love me, how did you intend to act tonight - on our wedding night?"

She flushed. It was so awkward to discuss the matter. "I will do my duty."

"Your duty? Is that all?"

"I will not refuse you, sir. I know the physical requirements of marriage."

"Know them?" he asked sharply. His eyes blazed at her. "Are you not a maid?"

"No, no," she said quickly to reassure him. "I am a maid. I only meant to say that my mother explained the process to me."

He seemed to be relieved to hear that, but his jaw remained tight. "And what did she advise?"

This was embarrassing to say out loud, but Elizabeth was determined not to be intimidated. She lifted her chin. "She told me that there is some discomfort at first, but that it improves. She also recommended that I close my eyes and try to think of something else." She smiled, hoping to infuse some humour into the conversation. "She said she often plans dinner menus."

He did not appear to be amused.

She watched with some trepidation as Darcy removed his robe and pulled the nightshirt over his head. In the flickering candlelight, she saw that like Mr. Higgins' son, he was trim and muscular as well.

"Well, Mrs. Darcy," he said coolly as he turned back to her. "I doubt you will be planning menus tonight."

CHAPTER FIVE

Elizabeth woke with a sense of warm satisfaction. She reached next to her and was disappointed to discover that her husband was not beside her. But no matter. Perhaps he was arranging for her breakfast. She stretched her arms and smiled, thinking of the night that had just passed.

Oh, Mr. Darcy, she thought. You amazed me.

The process of creating children had been so much more than she anticipated. She had never imagined feeling such a delicious, shuddering pleasure. No wonder the church talked about the sins of the flesh. Even now, thinking about his hands and his mouth, made her wish they were back together beneath the sheets.

She blushed, remembering all they had done.

Mr. Darcy had been so persuasive, so persistent.

She supposed she should call him Fitzwilliam now.

She felt a chill on her shoulders and realized she was still undressed. Where was her nightgown? She looked through the bedding and then saw the garment on the floor.

She slipped from the bed and pulled it back over her head. As much as her husband had seen all her charms by candlelight the night before, she was not brazen enough to be completely comfortable having him see her naked in broad daylight.

She went back under the covers and hugged herself for warmth, wondering when he would return.

When ten minutes had passed, she climbed out of bed to find her hair brush. She also washed her face and body with water from the basin, then returned to the bed.

She was surprised by how rested she felt. Her mother had been wrong. She had felt a momentary discomfort the night before, but overall the exercise had been delightful. She also had some aches this morning, but it was no more than she had felt the few times she had gone riding. She believed a hot bath would make her feel as good as new.

She waited but another half hour did not bring Mr. Darcy back.

She thought of the night before. Surely their actions had brought them closer, both physically and emotionally. She had fallen asleep in his arms, feeling safe and secure. He had been upset to learn that she had married him for his money, but now after all they had shared, he had to realize that she was beginning to care for him as well.

She smiled. Based on the last twenty four hours, she thought marriage to Mr. Darcy would be much better than she had anticipated.

There was a discrete knock at the door. "Come in."

It was Fisk. "Madam, are you ready to wake?"

Elizabeth tried to hide her disappointment. "Yes. Is Mr. Darcy awake?"

"Yes, ma'am. He has already had breakfast and gone for a morning ride."

Already eaten, without a word to her? Elizabeth did not know what she had expected of their honeymoon, but certainly not this. But then, her mother and father did not always eat breakfast together. Mrs. Bennet often ate in her room. She supposed she would have to learn the schedule for the household.

"I would like to eat breakfast in my room," she informed Fisk.

"Yes, ma'am."

When another maid brought in a breakfast tray, Elizabeth saw that there was a letter on it, addressed to her in Darcy's bold handwriting and sealed with wax.

She blushed, wondering what were his thoughts this morning. She waited until the girl had left to read it.

"Be not alarmed, Madam, on receipt of this letter, by the apprehension of it repeating our conversation of last night. I write without any intention of paining you by dwelling on facts that cannot be changed. What is done is done. We are lawfully wed and even if there were grounds for annulment, I would not put our private lives before the world for ridicule.

I trust it is in both our best interests to move forward, accepting the reality of our situation and presenting a civil front to society.

There is part of my conduct last night that I do regret. I was hurt and angered by your revelations, but that does not excuse my actions. I fully understand that now, in the light of morning, you may view me with abhorrence. I humbly beg your forgiveness.

I still look forward to having children with you, so I hope that in time, we can resume marital relations for that end. Although you may not accept my assertions today, I promise you that in the future, I will treat you with more gentleness and respect. And until then, I will not take advantage of you.

Your husband,
Fitzwilliam

Elizabeth could hardly believe what she was reading. With amazement she realized that he felt an apology was necessary. She was the one who had offended him. She should be begging his forgiveness for being so mercenary.

And obviously they had two different views of what had occurred the night before. He thought he should treat her with more gentleness and respect? That he had taken advantage of her?

Nothing could be further from the truth. They were man and wife. She had been surprised by the way he made her feel, but she had been a willing participant, especially as the night progressed.

She folded the letter and wondered where she should put it for safekeeping, away from the prying eyes of servants. "Fisk," she asked. "Is there a locked box I could have for my private correspondence and diary?"

"I will speak to Mr. Prewitt about it, ma'am."

"Thank you."

Until then Elizabeth chose to put the letter in with the ruby necklace and kept the key in her pocket. She readied herself for the day, then asked one of the footmen if Mr. Darcy had returned.

"I believe he is in his office, ma'am."

The day before, when Darcy had given her a tour

of the townhouse, he had shown her a small sitting room that he called his office. She walked there and saw him seated at a desk.

"Mr. Darcy?" she asked.

He looked up. His face was set as if in stone, his colour high. "Ma'am?"

"I have read your letter."

At this he stood and walked behind her to close the door so they could speak privately. "I believe the less said on that subject, the better."

"I disagree, but I promise I will not take much of your time." He stood stiffly, waiting for her to speak. She looked up at him, thinking that those were the lips she had kissed, the hair she had brushed with her fingers, but how different he looked in the light of day. He was nothing like the man who had once said he loved her. She said bravely, "As for last night, there is no need for an apology."

"I believe otherwise. You are less knowledgeable on the matter, but trust me, I know what respect is due to my wife."

Elizabeth recognized the wealth of ownership in the phrase 'my wife.' For better or worse, she belonged to him now. She blushed. "I did not mind, truly."

"You are too kind."

He did not believe her. And it appeared that he

looked back on what they had shared with distaste. She had heard before that men viewed the physical aspects of marriage differently than women, that they could lie with a woman without having any tender feelings.

She also remembered what he had said months before about his resentful temper. That his good opinion once lost was lost forever.

By marrying him for his fortune had she lost his good opinion forever?

The silence between them grew increasingly awkward. Finally she said, "Pardon me, I am sorry I bothered you."

"Elizabeth," he said calmly. "You may interrupt me at any time. I am at your disposal."

But apparently not in her bed.

She excused herself and left the room. She spent the rest of the day pretending to read or staring out the window at the street. Darcy did not seek her out.

At dinner he said, "Rather than stay in London for a few days, I thought it would be best if we go forward to Pemberley. Are you agreeable?"

What did it matter? She supposed he no longer wished to take her to view the sites in London or to take her shopping for clothes as he had mentioned earlier. He wanted nothing to do with her. She said, "That would be fine."

"Good. Please prepare to travel tomorrow morning."

They ate the rest of the meal in silence.

As she ate the delicate white flummery, normally one of her favourite desserts, Elizabeth began to envy her friend Charlotte. Mr. Collins might be a fool, but at least he spoke to her. Charlotte would never doubt for a moment what her husband was thinking.

* * *

Preparing to leave Darcy House was awkward. Elizabeth did not disclose any of her conversations with her husband, but she could tell that the servants knew something was wrong. Fisk, who had been so pleasant and good natured the day before, was now quiet and hesitant. One of the chambermaids looked as if she was going to burst into tears at any moment. Elizabeth wished she could think of something to say to make the situation better, but there was nothing she could say, so she merely focused on the tasks at hand. "Please use paper when packing my gowns so they will not wrinkle."

"Yes, ma'am."

As they travelled to Pemberley, Mr. Darcy was even more quiet than before, and he spent most of the time looking out the window or reading a book.

When they approached her new home, Elizabeth saw that the park was very large and contained a great variety of ground. They entered it in one of its lowest points and drove for some time through a beautiful wood. When the wood ceased, Elizabeth was able to see Pemberley House, situated on the opposite side of a valley.

She caught her breath. She had never seen a place for which nature had done more, or where natural beauty had been so little counteracted by an awkward taste. "It is lovely."

"I am glad you like it."

She flushed at his tone and hoped she would be able to express her approval without him always remembering that she had married him to gain access to his great estate.

They were met inside by Mrs. Reynolds, a respectable-looking, elderly woman, much less fine than the butler and housekeeper at Darcy House.

"We were not expecting you yet, sir. I hope you have not caught us out with half the work done."

Darcy said, "I doubt that, Mrs. Reynolds. I have never found your service lacking." He smiled and for a moment Elizabeth felt a twinge of sadness that his smiles were for his housekeeper now and not for her. "As for our haste, I found I could not wait to show

Pemberley to my wife."

Mrs. Reynolds said, "Welcome to Pemberley, ma'am. I hope you will be very happy here."

Elizabeth looked about the large entryway, noting the large windows, the ornate paintings on the ceiling and the statues on display. "It is magnificent. I look forward to seeing it all."

Darcy turned to her and said, "Forgive me, Mrs. Darcy, but if you wish a tour, I suggest that Mrs. Reynolds do the honours. Our travel today has fatigued me."

Elizabeth saw that Mrs. Reynolds was surprised, as she was herself. "I can wait until you are recovered," she said.

"Do not bother," he said. "I am certain she can tell you more about the tapestries and other history. If you will excuse me," he said and bowed. "I will see you at dinner."

Elizabeth stared at him as he walked away.

Mrs. Reynolds appeared as shocked as she, but she said gently, "The Master is normally of excellent health. Perhaps he has a headache?"

"Perhaps," Elizabeth said, making herself smile. She refused to cry in front of the servants.

"If you would like a tour, I would be happy to oblige," the housekeeper said.

Elizabeth tried to think what her mother would do in a similar situation. "Thank you, I would like that. But first, I would like a small tea and to freshen up after my travel. If you will show me to my room, please."

"Yes, ma'am."

Elizabeth walked upstairs to her new bedroom. She felt somewhat like the young woman in the tale of *La Belle et la Bete*. Was she to be abandoned to the great house, only to see the Master at dinner? In some ways, Mr. Darcy was acting like a beast.

Well, if he thought his silence was going to shame her, to break her spirit, he was mistaken. She was made of sterner stuff.

Her bedroom was a large, beautifully appointed room with a canopied bed and windows that looked out onto a rose garden below. "Lady Anne designed those gardens, ma'am," Mrs. Reynolds said.

Elizabeth said, "I wish I could have met her."

"Yes, it was a great loss when she died."

Elizabeth said, "If I had met her, she could have taught me how to be Mistress of Pemberley."

Mrs. Reynolds said, "We still have her diary and daybooks, if you would find that helpful."

"Yes, that would be most useful," Elizabeth said. "I'm afraid I grew up in a much smaller household. I will need your help to know what to do."

"I am completely at your service, ma'am," the housekeeper said. "We are all so happy that the Master has married and that Pemberley will have a Mistress again."

"Thank you."

Mrs. Reynolds nodded. "I will provide some refreshment and a bath, if you wish."

"That would be ideal, thank you."

She felt better after a bath and was determined to enjoy seeing Pemberley for the first time. Mrs. Reynolds was an effusive guide, giving her details about when the house was built and the dates and costs of various alterations and furnishings. They started in the dining parlour, a large well-proportioned room, handsomely fitted up. Elizabeth admired the room and went to a window to enjoy its prospect. She saw the woods in the distance, the river and trees scattered on its banks and the winding of the valley. She sighed. Even if Mr. Darcy could be unpleasant, his surroundings were superb.

As she continued her tour, Elizabeth was pleased to find the rooms lofty and handsome with their furniture suitable to Mr. Darcy's fortune. She admired his taste, finding it neither gaudy nor uselessly fine. Her new home had less of the splendour of Rosings Park, but more true elegance.

She was surprised in one room to see what appeared to be a miniature likeness of Mr. Wickham suspended over a mantelpiece. Surely Darcy would not have a picture of the man who had tried to elope with his sister. "Who is this?" she asked.

"George Wickham, ma'am. He was the son of the late master's steward. He was brought up by the late master's own expense but has now gone into the army. I'm afraid he has turned out very wild."

"Yes, so I hear," Elizabeth said.

Mrs. Reynolds was surprised. "Do you know the young man?"

"A little. He has recently been stationed at Meryton, near my home."

"Well," Mrs. Reynolds said stiffly. "I hope you did not see him often."

"No." Elizabeth did not want to talk of him further, so she motioned to the other miniature. "And this is Mr. Darcy when he was younger?"

"Yes. There is a finer, larger picture of him in the gallery upstairs. This room was my late master's favourite room, and these miniatures are just as they used to be then. He was very fond of them."

That explained why Wickham's picture was among them. "And here is Georgiana when she was little," Elizabeth said.

"Yes, she would have been eight years old."

"What a pretty child she was."

"And handsome now, as well," Mrs. Reynolds said loyally.

"Yes, she is a very handsome young woman," Elizabeth agreed. "I look forward to her arrival in a few more days."

Ms. Reynolds asked, "Have you heard her play the pianoforte?"

"Yes, she played a piece at Netherfield. She is very accomplished."

"You will find when she is home that she plays and sings all day."

"Sings?" Elizabeth said with surprise.

"Yes, when she sings she has no difficulty speaking." Mrs. Reynolds showed her a pretty sitting room that Darcy had recently refurnished for his sister.

Elizabeth admired the wall paper with a delicate fern design and the pale green curtains.

"And here is a new pianoforte that the Master just purchased."

Elizabeth ran her hand over the ornately carved wood. "He is a generous brother."

"Yes, you'll find that is the way with him. Whatever can give his sister any pleasure, it is sure to be done in a moment. There is nothing he would not do for her.

And for you, too, now that you are wed."

That remained to be seen. Elizabeth did not think he was feeling very charitable towards her at present, but she smiled, rather than respond verbally.

"I am so glad he found you," Mrs. Reynolds continued. "I was worried that he might not ever marry. I did not know if he would ever find someone good enough."

Mrs. Reynolds intended her statement as a compliment, but Elizabeth did not know if she meant that there was no one good enough to deserve him or that he would never think a woman was good enough.

The housekeeper added, "Pemberley has needed a mistress for many years. After Lady Anne died, the late master instructed us to continue as she would have wished, and we did our best, but occasionally situations arose that needed a woman's insight and supervision. And then when your Mr. Darcy inherited, he did the same."

"I will do my best to be a good mistress and I hope my husband will approve of my efforts."

Mrs. Reynolds said, "I am certain the Master will find nothing amiss. He has already spoken to me and to Cook on your behalf."

Elizabeth saw that although he was unhappy with her, he would do what he considered his duty. She asked, "Does Miss Darcy ever act as hostess?"

"No, ma'am."

She did not know if that was because of her stammer or shyness. "But of course, she is still quite young, although with her height, she appears older. Is she sixteen now?"

"Yes. Her birthday was in December."

As the tour continued, Mrs. Reynolds showed Elizabeth more of the principal bedrooms and then they entered the picture gallery. Elizabeth looked at the various family portraits, enjoying seeing Mr. Darcy's ancestors. But she was most interested in the portraits of Mr. Darcy.

There was one of him as a young child, standing beside his mother. "Is this Mr. Darcy?" she asked, looking at the young boy in a blue velvet coat with his hair in ringlets.

"Yes, he was about four years old. I was here when that was painted. The poor artist had a difficult time getting him to sit still."

Elizabeth smiled. "What was he like as a child?"

"He was always the sweetest tempered, most generous hearted boy in the world."

Elizabeth thought that the housekeeper was remembering him with rose coloured glasses. She thought there was a hint of wilful imp in his young smile. "It is almost a shame that we have to grow up," she commented.

Mrs. Reynolds frowned. "But Mr. Darcy is still the same, still good natured. I have never had a cross word from him in my life."

This was difficult to believe. Were they speaking of the same man?

But if what his housekeeper said was true, what did it say about her if she inspired him to sharp words? But then she thought of his reaction when he learned that she had married him for his fortune. Although angry with her, he had not raised his voice. He had spoken to her with a controlled reserve. He was not a man to display his temper. And in his letter, he had apologized where no apology was needed.

"He is a good man," Elizabeth said carefully.

Mrs. Reynold nodded. "Yes, and the best landlord, and the best master that ever lived. Not like the wild young men now-a-days, who think of nothing but themselves. There is not one of his tenants or servants but what will give him a good name. Some people call him proud; but I am sure I never saw any thing of it. To my fancy, it is only because he does not rattle away like other young men."

"No, he does not talk over much," Elizabeth agreed. "Although at times, I do wish he would say more."

"But what he does say is always worth listening to," the housekeeper said.

"True," Elizabeth said politely. "I believe you are his most staunch admirer, Mrs. Reynolds.

"Other than you, ma'am, I am sure," the woman demurred.

They walked to another portrait of Mr. Darcy. This was a solo portrait, painted only a few years previously by the look of it. He had a smile on his face that she remembered from when were engaged, but one she had not seen since she had offended him.

She stood several minutes before the picture in earnest contemplation.

Mr. Darcy had loved her when he proposed, and she believed that his feelings were sincere. He was unhappy with her now, but she refused to believe that he could never forgive her, never love her again.

If she wanted a happy marriage, she would have to repair the rift between them, but how?

She thought of her mother who whined and cried and complained about her nerves in an attempt to gain her husband's attention and sympathy. No wonder her father had hid himself in the library. No, she would not follow her mother's example.

She must find another way to regain his affection, but she did not want to be overly conciliatory.

She thought of Miss Bingley who had irritated Mr. Darcy with her constant flattery. He had pulled away from the adulation. She would not follow her example, either.

It would be wise to analyse why he had fallen in love with her in the first place.

Looking back, she believed he was sick of civility and the deference of officious attentions. He was disgusted with the women who were always speaking and looking and thinking for his approbation alone. She had roused his interest because she was different. Her impertinence had intrigued him, challenged him.

So if she wished to kindle his affections, she must maintain her emotional independence and be a woman worth winning.

She smiled and straightened her shoulders. There would be no more tears, no more feeling sorry for herself. She had married Mr. Darcy, she was the mistress of a large estate and surrounded by beauty. If her husband was displeased with her, which he was at present, at least he was civil and treated her with respect. She knew that her situation with a man less honourable could have been much worse.

That night at dinner Elizabeth put her new perspective into practise. She wore one of her favourite gowns in a pale yellow and she had asked Fisk to style her hair with ringlets in the back. "Good evening, husband," she said cheerfully.

"Good evening."

"I hope you are feeling better after your rest."

"I am, thank you."

"Mrs. Reynolds and I had a lovely time looking over Pemberley."

"I hope you found everything to your liking."

"I did, and I hope in time you will show me some of your favourite places. I particularly enjoyed the library. I have already taken several volumes to my room."

"Very good."

Elizabeth did not say anything for several minutes and the only sound was the quiet click of cutlery on the delicate china. After the course of venison and spiced mushrooms, she said brightly, "I hope you do not prefer to eat in silence, Mr. Darcy. Although I do not wish to sound like your aunt, Lady Catherine, I do not believe it is good for the digestion. Without conversation, one might eat too quickly."

He looked up at her in surprise and she smiled at him.

"Also, conversation is good for family unity as well, although I admit some of Kitty and Lydia's conversation was taxing."

"Then we are fortunate that they are not at our table."

Was that a hint of smile at the corner of his mouth? In the candlelight, it was difficult to tell. "Indeed," Elizabeth said and waited to see if her husband would continue.

He did not, so she persisted. "I thought you might share something about your day, or if there was nothing of interest there, that you might discuss your plans for the morrow." There, Mr. Darcy, she thought. I have thrown down the conversational gauntlet.

"If the weather permits, I will go riding tomorrow morning."

Ah, the weather again. This could be an amusing game to count how many times he referenced it. But she feared that if she sipped from her wine glass at every mention, she might become tipsy. "I have never learnt to ride well," she admitted. "I believe my father's mount was at fault, for it was such a large beast and I was young. By any chance do you have a gentle mare that would be good for me?"

"Georgiana's mare is gentle."

"Do you think she would mind sharing?"

"No, and the horse needs the exercise."

"Excellent. With whom should I speak to arrange lessons?"

"I will speak to Wheatley. He is the head groomsman."

"Thank you. You are most kind." She smiled at him. "You may relax now, Mr. Darcy. I am done with pestering you. That is sufficient personal conversation for the remainder of the meal, unless you feel compelled to add to it."

"Do you think I must be compelled to speak?"

"No. I just don't want you to feel obligated. Besides, if you have so little to say to me, perhaps it is best if you parcel it out in small amounts every day, so that you do not run short before the end of the week."

She tried to gage his reaction to her teasing, but his face was like a mask. She took a bite of the bread pudding. "This is delicious. Even so, Mrs. Reynolds informed me that Pemberley has used the same menus for the past eight years. Do you mind if I alter them?"

"No, do as you wish."

"Thank you. Also, Mrs. Reynolds has given me your mother's day books so I may learn how to fulfil my duties as Mistress of Pemberley."

"You would do very well to take my mother as a guide."

"I will do so, thank you."

* * *

The next evening after another day in which she wandered through the house looking for something to occupy herself, Elizabeth was surprised when Darcy actually began a conversation himself at dinner. He said, "I understand you went walking today."

"Yes, I did. The weather," she smiled for now she was talking about it as well, "was lovely and the grounds of Pemberley are beautiful. I walked around the short path by the lake. The gardener said it is a little more than two miles."

"You went by yourself."

"Is that a problem?"

"I would prefer if you took a footman or a lady's maid if you are going to walk beyond the view from the house, which would be the lawn and rose gardens."

Elizabeth frowned. "I walked by myself at Hunsford."

"Yes, and although I always enjoyed meeting with you, I was a little concerned about the safety or propriety of your actions."

Elizabeth was flabbergasted. "I am surprised that you lowered your standards to accompany me. What could you have been thinking?"

"I wanted to spend time with you."

His tone was flat and logical. She could not tell whether he was merely stating a fact or if he now regretted his prior emotions that had led to his proposal.

"I think you are being overly cautious. What can be the possible harm of my walking on the grounds of Pemberley by myself?"

"What if you became lost or if you had an accident?"

"I am not a child."

"If something happened, no one would know where you were."

"Then I will report to Mrs. Reynolds before I go. Would that satisfy you?"

He sighed. "I am not trying to be unreasonable. Pemberley is large. The odds of something untoward happening are small, but we do have an occasional poacher or a stranger passing through. I just believe it is more prudent to be wise than foolhardy. I don't let Georgiana go anywhere by herself. She is always accompanied by Mrs. Annesley or a maid."

"What if I were armed, would that reduce your fears?"

"Now you are being ridiculous. Your parents did not let you go to Meryton by yourself, did they?"

"No," she admitted. And her mother often fussed at her for walking to Lucas Lodge by herself.

He continued, "When you walked to Netherfield

when Jane was ill, I was surprised you had not brought someone with you. At the time I thought your father did not have sufficient servants to assist you. At least Jane came on a horse."

"It is unfair. Men can go wherever they please, whenever they please," Elizabeth said hotly. "And what about your tenant farmers' daughters or girls from the village? Do none of them walk alone?"

"I believe most of them try to go in pairs." He sighed. "I did not make the world we live in, Elizabeth. It is an uncomfortable fact that women are at a disadvantage in size and strength. I am trying to protect you."

She saw that she would lose this argument. "Very well," she said with poor grace. "I will take someone with me when I go for longer walks."

"Thank you."

They finished the meal in silence.

* * *

The first three days at Pemberley were unbearable for Darcy. He felt as if his heart would burst from his conflicting emotions. First, he was still angry that Elizabeth had married him for his fortune. She did not love him and had allowed him to express his feelings, playing him for a fool. And yet, part of him still loved her, and he grieved the loss of that dream.

Love her or hate her, he could think of no one else.

His feelings vacillated between hope that he might be able to win her affection and self disgust for his actions on the wedding night.

Would that he could erase those memories from his mind. He had thought only of his own desires. He knew better. His father had taught him that a gentleman must always be self-disciplined.

"As Master of Pemberley, you will be responsible for hundreds of lives. They will rely on your wisdom. You cannot be selfish or petty. When you are angry, maintain silence until you can speak civilly and solve a problem, rather than bursting out in a tantrum. Once said, words cannot be withdrawn or forgotten. It is better to remain silent. And if you are too angry to speak, take a walk."

Darcy had striven to follow those strictures his entire life, and yet with Elizabeth, he had let his passions override his reason.

When he saw her sitting across the dining room table, it was all he could do to talk civilly to her. He wanted to take her in his arms and beg her forgiveness, but he feared that once he did, he would kiss her again and he did not trust himself to act the gentleman. He knew that given the opportunity, he would take advantage of her again.

He thought at first that he could stay at Pemberley and limit his interactions with her, but he tossed in his bed at night, unable to sleep. Within a few days he thought it best that he leave until he could gain mastery over himself. He mentioned it at dinner. "I am leaving tomorrow for London and then travelling north to check on some of my other properties and investments."

"Do you wish me to go with you?"

"No, I want you to be here when Georgiana arrives."

"Do you know how long you will be gone?"

"No, but it could be several weeks or longer."

"Very well." She smiled as if she would not miss him. But why should she? She did not love him. Perhaps she would be relieved that she no longer had to speak with him.

All this introspection would drive him mad. He must keep himself busy, doing things that needed to be done.

"Is there a way to communicate with you while you are gone?" she asked.

That at least showed some level of care for him. "You may write to the Darcy House in London and if necessary, they will forward it to me."

That night he stood at the doorway that connected his room to Elizabeth's for nearly an hour. He heard the sounds of her preparing for bed. He heard her talking with her lady's maid. Eventually the room quieted and he knew she was alone. All he had to do was to knock on the door. She would let him in. She would not refuse him. She had said she would do her duty. Within minutes he could be back in her arms.

He reached for the doorknob but then held back. He would not return to her bed until he could treat her as she deserved. He must forget the night they had shared.

He turned back towards his own bed and was startled to hear a knock at the door. His breath caught in his throat. "Elizabeth?"

"Yes. May I come in?"

He stepped several feet away from the door so she would not know how close he had been. "Yes."

She opened the door and stepped inside. She was wearing a nightgown with a higher neckline and a robe that tied about her waist. Her hair was in a serviceable braid. She was beautiful. Darcy tightened his hands into fists at his sides to keep from reaching for her.

She said, "I am sorry to bother you, but I wanted to speak to you privately."

"You may." His mind raced. Did she want to lie with him?

She smiled. "Thank you. Since I do not know how long you will be gone, I thought it best to ask for some of my pin money."

The last thing he had expected her to mention was money, but then, he reminded himself, that was why she had married him.

"Is there something you wish to buy?" Even to his ears, his voice sounded harsh, awkward.

"No," she said. "But I might, and I believe it is best to be prepared for any eventuality."

"If you wish to buy anything in Lambton, they will send me the bill."

"Are saying that you will not give me any money?"

"No, of course not." He walked over to a desk and returned with a stack of bank notes. He counted out fifty pounds and handed them to her.

"Thank you." She reached up to kiss him on the cheek.

"Don't," he said sharply.

"Why not?"

"I will not pay for your favours."

"You do not have to pay for them. I give them freely."

He clenched his teeth, determined to put her temptation behind him. "Please leave. It is late and I must sleep to be able to get up early in the morning. I intend to leave before you wake."

From the high colour in her face, he saw that Elizabeth was offended. She said coolly, "Then if I do not see you before you leave, God bless you. Travel safely."

"Thank you. If you need to reach me, write to Darcy House. I will also write to inform you of my location."

"Very good. Good night, Mr. Darcy."

"Good night, Mrs. Darcy."

She returned to her room and closed the door between them with a loud slam.

Darcy stood for a moment and rubbed his hands on his face. What was wrong with him? He should have accepted her kisses, taking whatever she offered. He mentally cursed himself.

He was a fool.

CHAPTER SIX

Two days later, Elizabeth was pleased to receive a letter from Jane. It was dated a few days after her wedding. She quickly read through the introduction and Jane's well wishes. She then slowed to read more important news.

Mr. Bingley has proposed and we are to be married. Oh Lizzy, I am so happy. Father is pleased and Mother cannot contain her joy. Indeed, she had to spend a day in her room because of heart palpatations. Mr. Bingley has gone to London for a special license so we can marry quickly. Father's health seems to have rallied by the news and I hope he will be with us for many more months.

Elizabeth doubted that was possible, but she supposed it was not wrong to hope. She looked back at the letter.

Mr. Bingley says he loved me all the time, but in his modesty, he thought I did not care for him. He says we owe our happiness to your dear husband who told him that he thought I held him in regard.

So do thank your Mr. Darcy by whatever means you think best.

Elizabeth blushed. Her Mr. Darcy had no interest in accepting her gratitude in any form. It still stung that he had refused her kiss the night before he left. She continued reading.

I know it would be asking too much for you to return home for our wedding, but I wish that you could be here.

Write to me soon so I can bear your absence a little better.

And tell me all about your happiness. At least as much as you are comfortable sharing.

I will admit that I find the prospect of being a married woman daunting, but Mr. Bingley assures me that we will be the happiest couple in England.

Elizabeth smiled. Bingley was correct. She did not think there would ever be a couple more evenly matched and formed for happiness. Bingley and Jane were both so good, kind and patient. Bingley would never treat his wife with cold distain. He would not leave her without giving an estimate of when he would return.

The more Elizabeth thought of her husband ignoring her and abandoning her on their honeymoon, the more irritated she became. He had professed his love, but that love had not withstood a challenge. She was annoyed with him and with herself for even caring about it.

Now that Bingley had come up to scratch, there was no need for her to have sacrificed herself by marrying Darcy. However, she admitted, he would not have proposed to Jane if Mr. Darcy hadn't intervened.

But then again, Mr. Darcy had been the one to cause the trouble between Jane and Bingley in the first place. It would have been better if Mr. Darcy had never come to Netherfield at all. Mr. Bingley could have fallen in love with Jane and married her without any of the drama and turmoil. But would his sisters have conspired against Jane? It was a muddle, impossible to know what might have happened.

She supposed she must adopt her husband's attitude of what's done is done, and learn to live with the consequences.

Georgiana arrived within a week. She was not surprised by her brother's absence. "He often goes to London and rarely tells me why."

Elizabeth said, "I think gentlemen have the advantage in that respect. Can you imagine the uproar if you or I decided to leave on a moment's notice?"

"I know I could not," Georgiana said. "But now that you are m-married, can you not? My m-mother often travelled to London or to Rosings by herself."

"By herself?" Elizabeth questioned. "How is that possible?"

"She would go in her carriage."

"But she must have had servants."

"Oh, naturally. There would have been the d-driver, two f-footmen, and her lady's m-maid."

"And all that would have taken coordination with the staff. And my guess is that she would consult with your father before leaving."

"M-Most likely."

Elizabeth shook her head. "It is the way of the world. Men have more freedom. And once we are married, we are under their control."

"B-But m-my b-brother is a most reasonable m-man."

Elizabeth was not certain she could agree with that, so she said instead, "While he is gone, we shall do exactly what we wish. I have been talking with Cook and planning new meals. Do you have a favourite dish?"

"M-Mince pie."

"Excellent. We will have that tomorrow. And I would like to go to Lambton. Would you like to go shopping with me?"

Georgiana laughed at her exuberance. "I would."

"And there is one other thing. I would like to walk around Pemberley's larger path."

"A full ten m-miles? I am willing to take a p-pony cart, but I would not wish to walk it. It would take hours."

"I suppose you are right," Elizabeth said, disappointed that Georgiana did not want to accompany her. One of these days she would walk the entire path, but she did not want to inconvenience one of the maids for a whim, either. She smiled. "A cart ride would be fine."

Two days later, they took a carriage to Lambton and stopped at a milliner's shop. Since she knew her father would die soon, Elizabeth purchased a black bonnet and black gloves. If she were still at Longbourn, she would have some of her older dresses dyed black, but now that she was Mrs. Darcy, she decided to order a new black dress as well. A dressmaker took her measurements and said she would send an assistant to Pemberley when the gown was ready for a fitting.

That was another one of the benefits of being the Mistress of Pemberley, Elizabeth thought. Her mother would be impressed.

Georgiana bought some handkerchiefs and a tiny bottle of cologne. "For Mrs. Annesley," she said. This was one of first times in years that Mrs. Annesley had not accompanied her on an errand. Elizabeth noticed that Georgiana was very quiet in public, speaking only when absolutely necessary. A footman carried their packages.

On the way home, Elizabeth asked Georgiana her opinion. "I thought you were going to comment at the dressmakers, but then you thought better of it. Have I made a mistake? Do you think the dress will be hideous or does the dressmaker do poor work?"

"No, most of my clothing is m-made in London, but I have never heard anything against her. Indeed, all Lambton will be abuzz, discussing our p-purchases."

"I did not think of that," Elizabeth said. She had noticed her preferential treatment. She hoped they would not think Mrs. Darcy was a spendthrift.

"Yes, now that you are Mistress of P-Pemberley, everything you do will be a matter of great interest."

"How do you manage the attention you receive as Miss Darcy?"

Her sister-in-law shrugged. "It has always been that way. But my b-brother has tried to shield me from some of it. The only time I did not feel as if I was on d-display was a year ago when I was in Ramsgate. No one knew me. No one cared about my d-dowry."

Other than Wickham. Elizabeth said carefully, "I am sorry that trip did not end well."

"My brother told you about Mr. Wickham?"

"Yes."

Georgiana nodded. "I wish he would not worry about m-me, but I suppose that is imp-possible." She smiled. "I am wiser now."

"I am sure of it."

As if wanting to change the subject Georgiana then said, "I think your dress will be very p-pretty, other than being b-black. Do you think it is morbid to buy m-mourning clothes before they are needed?"

"Perhaps," Elizabeth agreed. "But I want to be prepared. I doubt I will be in the mood to go shopping after I receive the news."

"Mr. Bennet seemed better the last time I saw him," Georgiana said, encouragingly.

"That is what Jane wrote as well. Perhaps his situation is not as dire as we feared."

"I hope he will live a long time."

"So do I."

"At least he was there for your wedding."

Elizabeth heard the sorrow in Georgiana's voice and she was sympathetic. Poor Georgiana had lost both her parents. "Your brother will give you away at yours."

Georgiana shook her head. "I d-do not think I shall ever m-marry."

"Because of the stammer?"

She nodded.

"The right gentleman will not mind. Indeed, in the past few days, I have hardly noticed it."

Georgiana smiled. "You have a good heart."

Elizabeth smiled in return and they were both silent for a few minutes. Then Georgiana added, "I am glad my brother m-married you. For a while I was t-terrified that he might marry Miss B-Bingley."

"Oh no. Did you think he cared for her?"

"Not at all, but she was so p-persistent."

"She was that." And although it might be petty, Elizabeth was glad that Mr. Darcy had loved her rather than her rival. And no matter how unhappy she was with him now, she would never wish Miss Bingley upon him like a curse. He deserved better.

"She pretended to like m-me, but I knew that was false. She never waited for me to finish what I was saying."

Elizabeth said, "That must be very difficult."

"It is," Georgiana admitted. "There is so much I wish to say, but I speak so slowly that few p-people have the patience to truly listen."

"I hope I am a good listener."

Georgiana reached over and took her hand. "You are, thank you."

"And your brother, too."

Georgiana smiled. "He tries, but you know how he is. He only sees situations one way."

"Give him a chance," Elizabeth said, and realized that perhaps her advice should be directed to herself as well.

* * *

The next few days were uneventful, with Elizabeth gradually learning more of her duties about the house. Mrs. Reynolds had provided her a chart, listing all the servants so she could memorize their names and positions. In idle moments, Elizabeth wondered what Darcy was doing and whether he missed her. She wished he would return, if only for them to have an argument at dinner. Although Georgiana was a pleasure to talk to, she was more placid and never challenged her, never disagreed. The closest they came to a disagreement was discussing Childe Harold.

During one of their walks, they spoke about Jane

and her upcoming wedding to Mr. Bingley. Georgiana said, "A few years ago, I think Fitzwilliam considered Mr. B-Bingley as a potential husband for me. I am so glad he is going to m-marry your sister instead."

"He is not your ideal?"

"No, he is too calm, too polite. I would want a m-man with more passion."

Elizabeth agreed, but thought it not quite a proper discussion for her to have with her unmarried sister-in-law.

"I want a man who has run through Sin's long labyrinth."

Elizabeth said, "I know that Byron's Cantos are currently very popular, but I am not impressed. The hero sounds like a selfish rake to me."

"But consider the next lines: He *Had sigh'd to m-many though he loved but one, and that loved one, alas! Could ne'er be his.* He is so alone. He loves a woman he can never have. Does that not t-touch your heart?"

"What – that he seduces other women because he cannot have the one he wants? I do not find that romantic at all."

Georgiana frowned. "Perhaps you are right."

"I am surprised you read Byron. Does your brother know?"

"He has never censored my reading."

"Well, remember there is a great difference between poetry and reality."

"Yes, I know, but can you b-blame me for dreaming about a dark and d-dangerous lover?"

For an instant Elizabeth thought of Darcy, his lips on her throat and she shivered. "As long as he is safely between the pages of a book, that should not be a problem."

* * *

A few days later, Elizabeth received the mail and saw that she had another letter from Jane and that there was also a letter for Georgiana. There was no letter from Mr. Darcy, but then she had not been expecting one. He had only sent one brief note when he first arrived in London to let her know that he had travelled safely. She kept this letter locked with the other one with her ruby necklace.

She walked through the large house until she heard Georgiana playing the pianoforte in her sitting room. She stood back, waiting for Georgiana to finish. She did not want to distract her. Elizabeth looked around the room, thinking how quickly she had become acquainted with the magnificence of Pemberley. She no longer stared at the ceilings, amazed by the paintings of biblical and literary scenes by Verrio, or ran her fingers over the ornate wool carpets or silk curtains. She was no longer conscious of the liveried footmen standing in the hallways, ready to open the large, beautifully carved and gilded doors if the need arose. Georgiana finished the piano sonata and sighed, leaning her face on her hands.

"Herr Beethoven?" Elizabeth asked.

Georgiana looked up quickly. "Yes. It is one of my favourite pieces."

"You play so well. The last movement is so challenging."

Georgiana said, "I know I m-made some m-mistakes."

"Even so, it was lovely," Elizabeth said. "And so emotional, but then Herr Beethoven's compositions are often fierce."

"I agree," Georgiana said. "That is why I like it."

Elizabeth smiled at her. "I like it, too. They say he is not a happy man, but he creates works of such powerful beauty. I wish I could hear one of his symphonies with a full orchestra."

"Perhaps when we are next in London," Georgiana said.

"Oh, before I forget," Elizabeth said and handed her the letter. Georgiana recognized the handwriting on the envelope and smiled. She put it in the pocket of her day dress. "I will read it later."

"You must be a better correspondent than I," Elizabeth said, "Because you receive more letters." She had noticed that a day rarely went by without Georgiana receiving mail.

Georgiana said, "When I was younger, I attended a school in London and made m-many friends."

"Well, it is a compliment to you that they continue to correspond." Thus far, Elizabeth had only received letters from Jane and one from her friend Charlotte.

"I find writing much easier than speaking. I can express myself m-much more clearly without my stammer slowing me d-down."

That made sense to her. Elizabeth was glad Georgiana had some friends, even if they were at a distance. From what she understood there were few young women Georgiana's age in their part of Derbyshire and Georgiana did not have any close friends to visit.

Elizabeth took Jane's letter to her sitting room where she could read it in private and compose a reply.

Dearest Lizzy,

I am writing to tell you that our father has died.

Elizabeth took a deep breath. She had known this day was coming, but the news still brought tears to her eyes. She continued to read.

We knew he was ill, but had hoped he was improving. On Wednesday night, he took a sudden turn for the worse with pain and vomiting. As you know, Bingley had gone to London for a special license. We had planned to marry a week later, but with Father dying, we thought it best to marry immediately so we were married in a quiet ceremony Thursday morning. Father died a few hours later. He did not speak at the end, he merely breathed deep until he passed away. I think he was at peace.

Our mother is beside herself. I have written to Mr. Collins and he sent an express to say that they are on their way. At present our plans are for the entire family to come to Netherfield, but I know that is not a long term solution.

Caroline talks about going to London to stay with the Hursts, so we will be less crowded.

The rest of the letter was more of Jane trying to be positive about a sad situation.

Poor Jane to be married without the celebration and

recognition from their friends and to immediately face their father's death. She would not have much of a honeymoon with her mother and three sisters at Netherfield.

Jane did not ask it, but Elizabeth knew that she would like her to visit.

Elizabeth decided that she would go to Meryton and spoke with Mrs. Reynolds to coordinate the matter. Mrs. Reynolds was surprised at first that she would want to leave while Mr. Darcy was away.

"I will write and inform him," Elizabeth said. "I believe he will wish to join me in Hertfordshire."

"But to travel alone, is that wise?"

"Lady Anne's diary lists many trips she took by herself, particularly trips to visit her sister Lady Catherine de Bourgh."

The housekeeper said, "You are right. The late master and Lady Catherine did not always see eye to eye."

Elizabeth thought this was an interesting revelation, but she did not have time today to learn more of the matter.

Mrs. Reynolds said, "I will arrange for the footmen and driver. I assume you will take Fisk. How soon do you wish to leave?"

"In the morning."

"Very good, ma'am."

Before she left, Elizabeth asked Georgiana if she wished to join her.

Georgiana frowned. "Would you mind terribly if I d-do not? I have travelled so m-much lately and I was recently at Netherfield. They will need every empty bed they have."

"I will miss you," Elizabeth said. "You are becoming another sister to me."

They embraced.

"Write to me," Georgiana said.

"I will," Elizabeth promised.

* * *

Elizabeth went first to Netherfield. Jane was pleased to see her, but there were shadows under her eyes which showed how difficult the past fortnight had been. They sat in one of the sitting rooms that looked out over the garden. They talked briefly of their father, then the conversation turned to Jane's wedding.

Jane said she did not mind the rushed ceremony, as long as she and Mr. Bingley were lawfully man and wife.

Elizabeth asked, "Are you happy?"

"I cannot begin to express it. He is so kind, so thoughtful. As soon as father died, he invited everyone to come to Netherfield."

"But it cannot be easy to have our mother and sisters here. Do you have any privacy at all?"

Jane blushed. "We have managed to find some time to be together."

Elizabeth wondered what kind of lover Mr. Bingley was, but she would never embarrass her sister by asking directly. "Do you like being married?"

"Oh Lizzy, it is most exhilarating."

Elizabeth laughed. "It is, isn't it?"

Jane laughed a little as well. "So you and Mr. Darcy are happy together?"

Briefly happy together; unhappy now apart. It was impossible to answer, so Elizabeth prevaricated. "We have hardly seen each other. Mr. Darcy needed to visit some of his properties."

Jane was concerned. "I hope he is not having financial problems."

"No, as far as I know, his finances – our finances - are healthy." That would be ironic, if she had married the man for his money only to have him later lose it.

Their conversation was interrupted by Bingley's arrival. "Miss Elizabeth!" he said cheerfully, then quickly corrected himself. "Mrs. Darcy."

"Mr. Bingley," she said as he first took her hands, but then he smiled and pulled her into a quick embrace.

"You are my first brother," she said happily as he released her. "I am so glad to have you as part of my family now."

"Is Darcy here as well?"

"No, not yet," Elizabeth said. "I do not know his plans."

Bingley glanced quickly at Jane with a slight frown, then said, "Well, thank you for coming at this difficult time. I know your mother will appreciate it."

Elizabeth then rode a carriage to Longbourn, where she found the household in an uproar with Mrs. Bennet deciding which items she would take and which items needed to stay for the Collinses as part of the entail. "It breaks my heart to think of that scheming Charlotte Collins sitting in my dining parlour. If you had married him, Lizzy, we would not have to leave."

"But if I had married him, I could not have married Mr. Darcy," Elizabeth reminded.

Mrs. Bennet sniffed. "You are right, and I am glad you are so wealthy. But I shall miss Longbourn." She turned to Mary who had come to help with the packing. "You should have married Mr. Collins."

"Mama!" Elizabeth protested. "That is unfair."

Mrs. Bennet said, "I know. It is just so upsetting. I never realized how much I would miss Mr. Bennet once he was gone. I don't want to be a widow – old and forgotten, like an old shoe no one cares for."

Elizabeth said, "We will not forget you. Jane and I will see that you are taken care of."

She dabbed her eyes with a lace handkerchief. "If it weren't for Mr. Bingley, I don't know what would become of me."

Poor Jane. Elizabeth was glad that when her trip was over, she could return to Pemberley and not have to deal with her mother on a daily basis.

That evening, they were all at Netherfield. After dinner Mrs. Bennet retired early to her bedroom to rest. "My nerves have been exhausted."

Jane was a perfect hostess. "Would you like me to send up a maid with a tisane?"

"I don't know if it will do any good," Mrs. Bennet said. "But I will take it, thank you."

The rest of them moved to a sitting room. Mary played the pianoforte and Kitty and Lydia played cards, until Kitty accused Lydia of cheating. "I did not!" Lydia declared, throwing the cards on the table. "I don't want to play anyway." She pouted. "There is nothing to do! The militia are gone and Father is dead. There is nothing to live for. No balls or dancing for six months!" she wailed. "If only Father had let me go to Brighton."

Bingley glanced at Jane in a way that made Elizabeth think they had heard this complaint before.

"But you would have had to cut your visit short," Elizabeth argued, but Lydia did not listen to her.

"And you'll never guess what we heard from Aunt Phillips today," Kitty added. She and Lydia had spent the afternoon at their aunt's house rather than helping at Longbourn.

Kitty would have continued, but Lydia interrupted her. "Wickham has left the army. They say he ran off to London to avoid gambling debts. It is all Miss King's fault. If she had married him, he never would have been in such a position. Poor Wickham."

And fortunate Miss King, Elizabeth thought.

The next day, Jane spoke to her privately about Wickham. "Everyone is talking about him now that he has left Meryton. He has run up debts with nearly every tradesman in town, and," Jane blushed before adding, "Possibly despoiled many of the tradesmen's daughters. I can hardly believe it."

"I can believe it," Elizabeth said. "He cares for nothing but himself."

"Perhaps his debts made him desperate."

"It isn't desperation that makes a man seduce a young woman. It is nothing more than selfishness on his part and foolishness on hers."

"Well, I hope the reports of his misdeeds are exaggerated."

"You are too tender hearted," Elizabeth said. "The world is a wicked place and filled with conniving opportunists. But enough of Wickham. What should we do with Mama?"

CHAPTER SEVEN

Elizabeth's letter was forwarded twice to Darcy. It reached him when he was visiting cotton mills in Manchester. When he looked at the date, he saw that it had been written a more than a month earlier.

Dear Husband:

I hope this letter finds you well.

I write to inform you that I have left Pemberley to visit my family in Hertfordshire. My father has died and I believe I can be of use to them. As for the length of my stay, I assume it will be at least two months, but as you did not confirm your plans when you left, I will not confirm mine.

Georgiana did not want to travel and has stayed at Pemberley with Mrs. Annesley. I hope that meets with your approval.

If you could come to Hertfordshire, I would

appreciate it, but I make no request.
I wish for something better between us, Sir,
but that is your choice.
Elizabeth

Darcy was thoughtful as he reread the letter. She was not the only one who wished for something better between them. He did not want his marriage to be like so many in society – a sham of two people living a polite fiction, pretending to care, but in actuality ignoring each other as much as possible.

He felt that the time apart had strengthened his resolve. He should be able to converse with her without an excess of passion, whether that was positive or negative.

He would follow her to Hertfordshire to regain his wife.

A few days later, Bingley greeted him in the entrance of Netherfield. "Darcy, thank goodness you are here. What has kept you so long?"

Darcy did not want to explain his actions. "I am here now," he said calmly. "Where is Elizabeth?"

"Walking in the garden."

Darcy left his hat and gloves with the footman and walked out to the gardens. He saw her before she saw him. She was by herself. She wore all black from her bonnet to her leather boots, and the colour emphasized the cool smoothness of her skin. Her beauty was like a blow to his chest. Legally she belonged to him, but he did not know how she would respond.

"Elizabeth," he called out.

She turned, surprised and whatever emotion was on her face was quickly masked. "Mr. Darcy," she said calmly.

She had rarely called him Fitzwilliam. She stood stiffly, not offering even a hand in greeting. "Forgive me for taking so long," he said. "I received your letter just last week. I am sorry to hear of your father's passing."

"But you knew it was coming."

"Yes," he acknowledged. "How is your family?"

"Not well," she said. "The Collinses are at Longbourn and it is a daily sorrow to my mother. She spends much of the time in her bedroom."

"Would you like to walk?" he asked and offered his arm.

She hesitated, then placed her hand on his arm. "Where to?"

"Wherever you wish."

"That is a foolhardy promise," she said with a hint of her prior humour. "What if I wanted to go to London?"

"I would have to ask Bingley's cook for provisions."

She smiled at that. "That I would like to see. Mr. Darcy with a pack on his back. And a walking stick."

"And a hat like the gardener over there," Mr. Darcy added, motioning to an elderly man who wore a wide brimmed straw hat.

They walked in a leisurely manner and found themselves near Meryton. "I would offer to buy you refreshment," Darcy said. "But I came without a purse or hat."

"I don't think the proprietor would mind the lack of hat if your purse were heavy enough," Elizabeth said. "Or he could send a bill to Netherfield. I am well enough known that they would not mind. A greater concern is walking into town, past my Aunt Phillip's house. She keeps a steady eye on the front windows and will recognize me. We will offend her if we do not stop."

"If you wish to visit with her, I will not mind it."

She frowned. "This is a new Mr. Darcy. When did you become so complacent?"

"I want us to be happy together, Elizabeth. I have had ample time for reflection. You found me arrogant and selfish before, and you were correct. As a child, I was taught what was right, I was given good principles, but I was left to follow them in pride and conceit. I was spoilt by my parents and allowed to be selfish and overbearing. I was offended to learn that you married me for my fortune, but in truth, it is no more than I deserved. I had little else to please a woman worthy of being pleased."

Elizabeth said, "You are too harsh on yourself. You have many good qualities."

"Has the passage of time lessened your ill opinion?"

"My opinion was already improving when we were at Rosings. And since our engagement, you have been both kind and generous."

"Please forgive my ill temper at Pemberley."

"I do not mind an occasional ill temper, for indeed I can be angry myself. What I mind most is the silence. I would rather know why you are unhappy than to guess at your feelings. If I do not know what you are thinking, I presume the worst. Take your recent travels, for example. I was beginning to fear that I would never see you again."

"And that upset you?"

"A little," she said with a smile. "You are my husband, Mr. Darcy, and although I may dress like a widow, I do not wish to become one soon."

Darcy smiled. He would not press her further. He asked if she wished to speak with her Aunt Phillips, but she chose instead to turn back to Netherfield.

As they walked, they spoke of Jane and Bingley and their recent marriage. Elizabeth said, "I must thank you for speaking to Bingley on our wedding day. Without your encouragement, it might have taken him months to ask the question."

"It was the least I could do after my former interference. There was no time to apologize for concealing the fact that your sister was in town last winter. I suppose I could tell him now."

"But what would be the benefit?" Elizabeth asked. "They are happy. But if you wish to confess, I am certain he will forgive you quickly."

"Yes, his temper is much gentler than my own."

"But you seem to have forgiven me."

"What is there to forgive?" he asked. "Your father was dying. You did what was best to help yourself and your family. Perhaps if I were in your situation, I would do the same."

"What, if Pemberley was mortgaged and you were destitute?"

"And if I were a woman."

Elizabeth bristled. "Do you hold women to a lesser standard of behaviour?"

Darcy smiled. This was the woman he loved, who would challenge his statements. "No, I am merely acknowledging that women have fewer choices. And perhaps I would have married an heiress to boost my fortunes. If she were as pretty as you."

Was that a blush he saw on Elizabeth's cheek? She said calmly, "Now you sound like Colonel Fitzwilliam."

"Ah, my cousin Richard. For a few weeks at Rosings, I feared he would win your hand."

"No, he merely flirted with me."

"His loss was my gain."

They walked on and Darcy asked about Georgiana. "How is she? I have written to her, but only received two letters while I was gone."

"She was well when I left Pemberley. I have received a letter from her since my arrival, but it contained little news."

He sighed. "She has such a quiet, uneventful life. I am hoping that you can convince her to attend the Season next year."

"She is still young," Elizabeth reminded.

"Then the year after."

Elizabeth smiled, but did not comment.

"What?" he asked. "What are you thinking?"

"You are determined to make her happy, but what if the things you plan will not make her happy? Attending the Season may be a treat for most young women and an ordeal for her. Not everyone is the same. There is no one route to happiness. If you wish her to mix socially, perhaps you would do better by arranging some house parties."

Darcy smiled ruefully. "And that is why I need a wife."

Elizabeth laughed. "Indeed. I am a font of wisdom."

At that moment, Darcy felt a great desire to kiss her, but he restrained himself and instead, he merely patted her hand. He was so glad that they were talking, hopefully building their relationship, and he did not want to rush his fences.

* * *

When they returned to the house, Elizabeth excused herself to meet with her family and Darcy went in search of Bingley. He found him dozing in the library. Bingley sat up and yawned. "Pardon me, Darcy. Hello. I was taking a nap. Did you have a good walk with Elizabeth?"

"Yes, and I want to talk to you about her mother."

"Ah, Mrs. Bennet," Bingley said. "She is having a difficult time."

"I can imagine how taxing it has been for you to have all the Bennets here during what should have been your honeymoon."

"I don't mind."

"You are a saint, but you don't have to become a martyr. Do you really want your mother-in-law under your roof for the next year?"

Bingley blanched.

"I thought not," Darcy said. "Let me take care of it. We will rent a nearby location until the official mourning period is over, and then we will reassess."

They spent the next half hour discussing possible properties and devising a plan to introduce the topic to their mother-in-law. "I don't want her to feel that we are throwing her out," Bingley said.

"Then let your wife bring it up. Jane will know how to handle it delicately."

"Yes, you are right." Bingley yawned again and ran his hands through his hair. "Forgive me, I did not get enough sleep last night."

Darcy asked, "Are you ill?"

"No, I am recently married," Bingley said with a smile. "You know how that is. And my wife did not get enough sleep, either, but she at least has the option of sleeping in. It is not fair, Darcy. No one says a word if the lady of the house does not rise before noon."

Darcy frowned. "You should not bother your wife, disrupting her sleep."

"What if she is the one bothering me?"

Darcy could not believe what he was hearing. "Are you saying that Jane Bennet – I cannot believe it. She is one of the most ladylike women I have met in my life."

"How does that have anything to do with it?"

Darcy was surprised he had to say it out loud. "A well-bred young woman does not enjoy marital relations."

Bingley laughed. "Who told you that?"

Darcy was offended. "My father."

"Has it never occurred to you that your father could be wrong?"

Darcy blinked, then laughed at his own obtuseness. "No."

"I am sure your father was a most excellent man," Bingley said quickly. "And no doubt he gave you advice based upon his own experiences. But that does not mean he was infallible." Bingley shook his head. "I cannot believe I am giving you advice on such a matter."

"Apparently I need it," Darcy said ruefully. He could not believe it, either. Had Elizabeth been telling the truth when she said she did not mind what they had done? Could she have enjoyed it?

"Do not take my word only," Bingley said. "Even the church approves of it. Think of the words of the marriage ceremony. We are supposed to worship our wives with our bodies."

"I never thought of it that way."

Bingley said, "You must do as you see fit, naturally, but I think you may be denying yourself. Also, what does it matter what anyone else thinks? This is a matter between you and your wife. No one else needs to know, and indeed, I don't wish to know the particulars."

Darcy held up his hand. "I have no intention of giving specifics." He refused to be like a foxed gentleman at one of the clubs, boring an audience with his sexual exploits. "Now, if you will excuse me, Charles, I will let you return to your nap. You have given me much to think on."

* * *

Later that afternoon, Darcy found Elizabeth sitting with her mother and Jane. Mary was playing the pianoforte. He sat, joining the conversation with them for several minutes, then asked Elizabeth if she would like to go for a walk.

"Another?" she asked.

"Yes, for I know how much you enjoy walking."

She looked at him closely, as if trying to discern his meaning, then agreed. He walked with her in the flower garden and escorted her to a stone bench outside view of the house. He sat beside her and took her hand in his.

She waited for a long moment as he was quiet, then she said, "I see you are determined to increase my anticipation by your silence."

"No, I am merely thinking how to explain myself without looking a fool."

Elizabeth laughed at this. "Are we not all fools now and again?"

Darcy nodded. "As Puck declares." He took a deep breath and continued, "I want to start over with you, Elizabeth. As if today was our wedding."

"We cannot turn back time, but I do believe we should think of the past only as it gives us pleasure."

"That is a promising philosophy. I hope you will not have to exercise it regularly with me."

"That is up to you and how many good memories you wish to create."

"I would like to create a good memory right now." He reached over to touch her cheek.

"I am willing."

Darcy looked deep into her eyes, humbled by her forgiving attitude. He knew he did not deserve her. She was a precious jewel as her father had said, and he would spend the rest of his life cherishing her.

He leaned forward for a kiss.

She was so soft, so warm and accepting. He pulled her closer and deepened the kiss. Her hands were first on his shoulders, then around the back of his neck. He felt her smile, breaking the connection, and he drew back. "What is it? Is something wrong?"

"No, not at all," she assured him. "I was merely thinking that it is easier to kiss you when you are not wearing a cravat."

He drew his breath in sharply.

"Have I shocked you?" she asked.

"No," he said quickly, although to some degree she had shocked him. He kissed her again. It might take some time for him to completely forget his father's admonitions, but he was not going to let them stop him from enjoying his wife.

Eventually, they heard someone else in the garden walking up the gravel path and they separated, both of them breathing heavily. Elizabeth reached up to smooth her hair. Darcy squared his shoulders and brushed his coat.

A footman appeared. "Mr. Darcy. Mrs. Darcy. Mrs. Bingley wishes to remind you that dinner will be within an hour."

Darcy nodded. "Thank you. Tell her we will be there."

"It is a good thing we are married, Mr. Darcy," Elizabeth whispered as the young man left. "Otherwise, I would be compromised."

Darcy said, "I would like to compromise you."

Elizabeth laughed. "Perhaps later."

CHAPTER EIGHT

Fisk commented to Elizabeth that she appeared in better looks that evening as she helped her dress for dinner. Elizabeth blushed, thinking of the time she had spent with Darcy – actually kissing Darcy. For the past few weeks, she had been telling herself that she did not miss him, that she did not care for him, and then today when she saw him again, all her good intentions melted away like snow on a warm Spring day. She should be appalled by her fickleness, but all she could think was that he had returned, and he seemed to love her again. This time she would value his devotion. She said lightly, "I believe it is from the fresh air. I took several walks today."

"Remember your parasol," Fisk said. "You don't want to become tan with all the sun."

At dinner that evening, Elizabeth only had eyes for Mr. Darcy. She watched him, amazed by his civility as he listened to the complaints of her mother and the idiocy of her sisters. Kitty and Lydia had spent the day with Maria Lucas and they wanted to repeat the town gossip.

Elizabeth listened as Jane suggested the possibility of her mother setting up her own household. When her mother protested that it would cost too much, Darcy said she did not need to worry about that.

Mrs. Bennet brightened. "I would like to be in my own place. Not that I don't appreciate you, Mr. Bingley. You are most kind, and Netherfield is all that is lovely, but I need my own kitchen, Mr. Darcy."

Elizabeth bit her tongue to hide a laugh. Her mother did nothing in the kitchen other than give orders.

Darcy said, "Mr. Bingley and I were thinking you might like the great house at Stoke."

"No, the drawing room is too small."

"Mama," Jane interjected. "You will not be hosting parties this year, perhaps it will be large enough for the present."

"Or Ashworth," Mr. Darcy suggested.

"Oh no, I could not bear to be ten miles from Jane."

"What about Purvis Lodge?" Bingley asked.

Mrs. Bennet shook her head. "No, the attics are dreadful."

"Then the house at Stoke may be best," Jane reminded. "It does have lovely gardens."

Mrs. Bennet said, "Haye Park would be ideal, but I doubt the Gouldings would quit it." She sighed. "I miss Longbourn. If Mr. Bennet had not died, I would still be there and I would not need to think of moving. It breaks my heart to hear what Mrs. Collins has done. Mr. Darcy, do you know that she has replaced the paper in the breakfast room?"

Elizabeth had been hearing about this for days, but it was the first time Mr. Darcy had heard it.

To his credit, he took the news seriously. He merely nodded and said sagely, "Unfortunately, it is to be expected. A new owner does not always share the taste of the previous owner."

"Too true," Mrs. Bennet said with a sniff. "No one appreciates all that I've lost."

Elizabeth said, "No place will be as comfortable as Longbourn, but you must live somewhere, and I know you value your independence, being able to command your own staff."

"Perhaps I should stay at Netherfield," Mrs. Bennet said. "It will be so expensive to move."

Darcy said, "Think nothing of it, ma'am. All the expenses will be my gift."

Mrs. Bennet cried, "Thank you, Mr. Darcy, you are

too good."

"It is the least I can do to honour your husband." Darcy glanced at Elizabeth and smiled.

Elizabeth's heart softened. He was a good man, and she loved him. The realization surprised her. Her feelings for him had been growing so gradually, it was difficult to know when it first began, but for all her starts and stops, she loved him now. What had begun as a marriage of convenience had somehow changed to a love match.

"My poor, dear husband," Mrs. Bennet said. "Mr. Bennet was the dearest man, the best husband. I never heard a cross word from him in twenty-four years of marriage."

At this, Lydia rolled her eyes and Kitty giggled.

"It is true," Mrs. Bennet protested. "Lizzy, tell Mr. Darcy."

"My father was not a perfect man, no one is, but he did love my mother in his way." As I love you, she thought and hoped he could read the message in her eyes.

"There," Mrs. Bennet said triumphantly. "Just as I said."

Jane interrupted to speak of the house at Stoke again, the conversation shifted, and plans were made to make enquiries the next day with an estate agent.

After dinner Mary played the pianoforte. Darcy played a game of chess with Bingley. Elizabeth sat with a book on her lap.

After the game, Darcy rose to his feet. "If you will excuse me, Bingley, I would like to retire early. I am weary from my travelling."

"And I will join you," Elizabeth said. "Good night, Mama."

As they walked up the staircase to their bedrooms, a footman approached. "An express for you, Mr. Darcy."

"Do you mind if I read it now?" Darcy asked Elizabeth.

"No, for it might be important."

She watched as he opened the letter and scanned its contents. His face grew pale. "What is it?"

"It is Georgiana. She has eloped with Mr. Wickham."

"But how? How did he reach her?"

"Apparently they have been corresponding by letter. One of her London friends was an accomplice."

Now all those letters made more sense. "But what has been done?"

"I don't know. They won't get far without funds. Mrs. Reynolds says that Georgiana has taken some of her jewellery."

"I can't believe it."

"I assume she plans to sell them and the only place to do that is London. Perhaps that will slow them down a few days."

"When do you plan to leave?"

"Tonight. I will take extra drivers so we can drive straight through."

"Take me with you," Elizabeth said. She did not want to lose him again now that they were finally in accord. "Perhaps I can help with Georgiana."

"I am afraid you will slow me down. This will not be a leisurely journey. I will only stop to exchange the horses. I will sleep in the carriage."

"I do not need to be pampered, Darcy."

He looked at her. "All right, then. If you can pack within a half hour, you may come."

Elizabeth hurried to her bedroom. "Fisk!" she called out.

In the end, it took nearly an hour to have a portmanteau and trunk packed, but Darcy waited. Elizabeth gave quick farewell to Jane, and they were off. "Try to sleep," Darcy said. "It will be an uncomfortable ride."

"Poor Georgiana," Elizabeth said after a while. "What can she have been thinking?"

"Wickham is persuasive and she has always been sympathetic to him."

"And she has been reading Byron."

Darcy swore under his breath. "I thought she had more sense."

"I should not have left her at Pemberley. I should have stayed or insisted that she come with me to Netherfield."

"No, she is my sister, my responsibility. I should have stayed instead of leaving in a temper."

Elizabeth said. "Perhaps we could have stopped her, but assigning guilt will not find her. Where do you think she is?"

"Mrs. Younge now runs a boarding house. If Wickham is in town, she will know of it. And if he has left, she might know the route he took."

"With their head start, do you think you will be able find them in time?"

"I don't know, but I must try."

* * *

They arrived at Darcy House in the middle of the night. Elizabeth went upstairs to her room, while Darcy sent word to a Bow Street runner requesting his assistance.

Elizabeth slept and woke late for breakfast. When she came downstairs, she saw Darcy, shaved and dressed in a new waistcoat. "Did you sleep at all?" she asked.

"A few hours. I have spoken to Mrs. Younge and she will give me Wickham's address for a fee. She said she may need a day or two to procure it."

"Do you believe her? What if she is protecting him, allowing them extra time to escape?"

Darcy shook his head. "She is no longer an accomplice. He left her with a babe, recently born and died, and she is motivated merely by money."

"Wickham certainly leaves disaster in his wake."

"Yes, and my sister thinks he is romantic."

Darcy went to his bank to withdraw funds and spoke to several posting houses to see if Wickham had procured transportation. The Runner was going to all the pawnbrokers and money lenders to trace the jewellery.

By nightfall, there was still no news. Darcy did not want to eat, but Elizabeth convinced him that he needed to preserve his strength. They sat across the table from each other, both lost in their thoughts.

Darcy said, "I don't know whether I should go to Gretna Green to try to stop him there or hunt him down in London."

"There is no way to know which would be best. And in Scotland, they could go to any one of a dozen villages. Once they are past the border, it does not matter where they stop. Anyone can marry them."

"I wish there was a way to stop and search everyone travelling the Great North Road."

Elizabeth said, "Even if there was a way to alert the newspapers, that would still take time."

"And I do not want our family name in a newspaper." Darcy sighed. "If only my mother had not died. Obviously my sister needed a steadying female hand – more than I could give her."

Elizabeth thought of the Scottish nursery rhyme: if wishes were horses, beggars would ride.

That night, another maid assisted her, helping her get ready for bed. Fisk had remained at Netherfield. After the young woman left, Elizabeth could hear Darcy pacing in the adjoining room. She waited half an hour, then knocked on the door.

"Come in."

He was dressed for bed as well, in a nightshirt and robe. His hair was dishevelled as if he had run his hands through it. "Is something wrong?" he asked.

"No," she assured him. She walked up to him, wrapped her arms around his waist and rested her head on his broad chest. "I could hear that you were still awake."

Darcy stood stiffly for a moment, then as she continued to hold him, he relaxed and let his breath out with a shudder. "I don't want to bother you."

"It is no bother," she said. "Remember, marriage is for our mutual society, help and comfort, both in prosperity and adversity. Right now we are in the midst of adversity. Where else should I be?"

He smoothed her hair with one hand while the other drew her close. "Thank you."

After a long moment in which Elizabeth felt his heart beating, he said, "What if Georgiana –"

She reached up and put her hands to his lips. "Shh, Fitzwilliam," she said. "Save your worries for tomorrow."

He kissed her fingers, then reached down and kissed her lips.

Elizabeth sighed and drew him closer, She stood on tip toe and wrapped her arms around his neck.

They kissed several more times, then without words, he lifted her gently and carried her to his bed.

Much later he lay silent, almost asleep, his breathing slow and steady, and Elizabeth watched him in the flickering firelight. She felt truly married now, for marriage was more than passion. It was the mutual care they had for each other.

She did not know if they would be able to find Georgiana and stop her from marrying Wickham. In truth, she was angry with her sister-in-law. How could she be so foolish?

But hopefully they would learn more information in the morning. She turned on her side and the movement made Darcy stir. He wrapped his arm around her. "Do not leave me, Elizabeth," he murmured.

"I won't," she promised. One of these days she would tell him how ardently she admired and loved him, but tonight she would let him sleep.

* * *

They heard from Mrs. Younge by noon the next day. Elizabeth accompanied him to meet with her. Mrs. Younge, who had seemed a villainess from her prior behaviour, was a sweet, genteel young woman who looked only a few years older than Jane. It was another testament to Elizabeth that looks could be deceiving. She still found it difficult to believe that Georgiana had been hiding a tendre for George Wickham. She had seemed like a sweet, shy girl, not an adventuress.

Within an hour, money had exchanged hands and Darcy had the knowledge from Mrs. Young that he wanted. "It is not a good part of town," Darcy told Elizabeth. "Do you still wish to come, or would you rather wait at Darcy House?"

"I might be of assistance with Georgiana."

"As you wish. But I will make certain our coachman

and footman are armed."

"Do you think Wickham will be dangerous?"

"He may be desperate."

They found the eloping couple in a dirty hotel. The room had one bed and a table with the remains of a meal and an empty bottle of wine. Wickham was in his shirtsleeves. Georgiana was dressed, but her hair hung down, unstyled. Wickham smirked. "We meet again, Darcy," he drawled. "But this time I managed to keep Georgiana for a few days."

Darcy ignored him. "Georgiana, it is time for you to come home."

Georgiana stood her ground, angry and defiant. "I am not coming home. There is nothing you can d-do. I love him and we are going to get m-married, with or without your consent."

"Then you should have gone directly to Scotland."

"We are going there as soon as we can, but Wickham had to t-take care of business."

"Pawning your jewels? Why would you want a man who does not even have the means to hire a carriage?"

Georgiana flushed red. "I love him. I don't care about m-money."

Elizabeth interjected. "Do you know what will happen if you marry him without a settlement agreement? All of your money becomes his and there are no provisions for you. Do you trust that he will care for you?"

"W-Wickham loves me. He has always loved me."

Elizabeth asked, "What about Miss King? Did he love her, too?"

"He never cared for her."

Elizabeth was appalled by her wilful ignorance. She would believe what she wanted to believe. In some ways, she sounded like her sister Lydia.

Wickham said, "You will want a wedding, Darcy. Georgiana and I have been living as man and wife in every sense of the word."

"You blackguard," Darcy growled and came after him as if he would choke him.

Georgiana pulled at his arms. "Don't hurt him."

Darcy threw Wickham up against the wall. Elizabeth said, "If you hurt him, it will only make her think he's Romeo."

Darcy stepped back, releasing Wickham who sank to the floor, sitting against the wall. Darcy said, "Georgiana, you must come home."

"If you t-take me home, I will run away again," Georgiana said.

Wickham smiled up at her but did not make the effort to stand.

Darcy's face was red with anger. His hands formed fists at his sides.

Elizabeth said, "There must be a solution."

Darcy growled. "What? I cannot in good conscience let her marry him."

"But she says that if you do not agree, she will run away again. Can you keep her locked up for the next few years?"

"Yes, I can. And I will," Darcy said firmly.

Georgiana burst into loud, angry tears.

Darcy turned to Wickham. "And I will have you prosecuted for kidnapping."

Wickham shook his head. "You don't want the scandal. No one would ever marry her. No one wants used goods."

Darcy looked thunderous, but he kept his jaw clenched. "Elizabeth?" he said tightly. "What do you suggest?"

Elizabeth looked at Wickham. He was hardly charming now. He was an unwashed scoundrel, preying on the tender feelings of a girl. She looked at Georgiana, tearstained and distraught, but underneath that, she had a strong will. "Why do you love him?" Elizabeth asked.

"He has always cared for me, even when I was a child. H-He has always loved me. He listens to me."

The last sentence nearly broke Elizabeth's heart. She looked at Darcy, seeing her pain reflected in his eyes. "Perhaps it is best if they do marry," she said quietly.

"What?"

"Not right away," Elizabeth said quickly. "Consent to an understanding only. And if they still love each other when Georgiana is eighteen, let them marry."

"But that's t-two years from now!" Georgiana protested.

"Actually, only a year and a half," Elizabeth reminded. "If your love is strong enough, you can wait. Personally, I don't think Wickham will wait. If his interest in you is only financial, he will find someone else."

"Don't listen to her," Wickham said. He spoke to Darcy. "This is absurd. "What if there is a child?"

"If there is a child, then plans may change," Elizabeth said.

"I hope I am with child," Georgiana said hotly.

Darcy looked as if she had struck him.

Wickham laughed, "Admit defeat, Darcy. Your little sister loves me. She wants me."

"Lot of good that will do you at the bottom of the Thames."

"Are you threatening me? Would you commit murder?"

"Do not tempt me." Darcy glared at him, but then

said finally, "I will agree to this plan under two conditions."

Wickham looked wary. "What conditions?"

"First, you will transfer to a regiment in the North. And second, Georgiana must attend a Season in London." He spoke to his sister. "I want you to see what you would be giving up to marry him."

Wickham protested. "I can't afford to transfer. I have debts."

"Make a list of your debts. I will settle them and pay for the new commission."

Wickham looked relieved as he considered this information.

Georgiana saw it and cried, "It is too long to wait."

Wickham smiled. "No dearest, it is best. It will give me time to prove to your brother that I am worthy of you." He then kissed her hand in a gallant gesture.

Elizabeth kept a tight grip on Darcy to keep him from retaliating.

The next two weeks were unpleasant, but as Elizabeth often reminded Darcy, they were ultimately better than they could have been. They first took Georgiana back to Darcy House. Darcy spent the next few days with his banker and his solicitor setting up the arrangements with Wickham. The Bow Street Runner recovered the jewellery Wickham had pawned.

Within a week Georgiana had her monthly courses, which relieved both her and Darcy, and ten days later, Wickham left for Newcastle. Georgiana cried for three days, refusing to leave her bedroom, but eventually she was lured out by the promise of a trip to the theatre and shopping.

Darcy did his best to be civil to his wilful sister, and Elizabeth reminded him that she was still very young and that they had over a year for her to fall in love with someone more suitable.

Darcy added, "And we can always hope that some angry husband kills Wickham in a duel."

After one particularly trying day with Georgiana, he spoke to Elizabeth at night when they both lay in her bed. "I am sorry that I ever maligned your younger sisters, darling. None of them have run off with a fortune hunter."

"Only because they did not have a fortune to tempt anyone. I don't think Kitty or Lydia would be any wiser than your sister in the same situation."

Darcy sighed. "It is enough to make me never want to be a father. Or at least to never have daughters."

"Never?" Elizabeth said. She propped herself up on one elbow to look at him more closely. "That could be a problem."

Darcy frowned. "What are you saying?"

"I do not believe we can choose the sex of our child."

"Our child? Are you speaking hypothetically?"

Elizabeth smiled. "No, sir."

"But how, when? We have not been married long."

"Long enough," she said flatly. "I believe I conceived on our wedding night."

"That is wonderful news," he said and kissed her. "Are you well? Are you feeling poorly? Is there anything I need to do?"

"I am fine," she assured him. "All you need to do is to love me."

"Done, madam," he said and kissed her.

EPILOGUE

Elizabeth sat in the morning room, writing a letter to Jane while her son Bennet was napping. How she loved being his mother. He was an intelligent, beautiful little boy, just learning to walk. He could say a few recognizable words and Darcy teased that he was already speaking in complete sentences, merely in an unknown language.

Jane was expecting a child as well. She and Bingley lived only thirty miles from Pemberley now. They had stayed at Netherfield only a twelvemonth and then Bingley had bought an estate nearby. Instead of going with them, Mrs. Bennet had accepted Darcy's offer of renting a house in London. She was tired of living within the shadow of Longbourn and wished to make new friends and help her three remaining daughters find husbands.

Elizabeth hoped her sisters would be more

successful than Georgiana. Her sister-in-law had enjoyed her Season in London earlier that year. Many gentlemen found her and her fortune enchanting, as Elizabeth had anticipated, and their attentions had made Wickham less desirable. Darcy discouraged the fortune hunters and Georgiana could not make up her mind among the remaining suitors, so she had returned home, somewhat discouraged. "They are all so b-boring."

"Perhaps you'll find someone better next year," Elizabeth had said.

Darcy had reminded his sister that getting married was not a race. "Better to wait until someone superior comes along."

Elizabeth looked up from her writing desk to see Darcy standing in the doorway. She smiled at him in greeting, then noticed the opened letter in his hand and the strange expression on his face. "What news?" she asked. "Is that a letter from Bingley or my Uncle Gardiner?"

Mr. Gardiner often wrote to her husband now. Darcy had invested in his business, with positive results. And a month before, Mr. and Mrs. Gardiner had visited Pemberley and Lambton. Elizabeth was glad Darcy was finally getting to know some of her favourite relations.

Darcy said, "No, it is from Georgiana."

Elizabeth frowned. "I don't understand."

"Nor I, actually. It seems she has eloped again."

Elizabeth gasped. "With Wickham?"

"No, thank goodness. With Mr. Dodd."

"Mr. Dodd?" He was the portrait painter who had recently finished portraits of her and little Bennet and a single one of Georgiana. "Heavens," Elizabeth said. "What do we do now? I don't think I can go with you to chase her down. Not with Bennet."

"I think we let her go."

"What?"

"Consider this. She is almost eighteen. If she doesn't marry Dodd, who knows what her next choice would be?"

Elizabeth was not as sanguine. "What do you know of the man? I thought he was well mannered and quiet."

"He is. And you know he is talented. With the right introductions, he could be the next Reynolds."

Elizabeth had been pleased with the portraits, but that didn't mean she wanted him as a relation. "What of his character? Will he make a good husband?"

"A better question is whether she will make a good wife."

Elizabeth gave a little laugh. "The poor man."

"I know. I feel a little sorry for him. He has no idea what he is getting." Darcy shook his head. "My guess is that Georgiana instigated this adventure. "

"You may be right."

"At least they have enough money for the journey. I paid him yesterday."

"Then perhaps she has learned something in the past year."

"I hope so. But enough of Georgiana and her melodrama. She has her own will and I must let her exercise it. I just hope she will be happy."

Elizabeth looked at the man she loved so dearly. He had learned something in the past year as well. Darcy at Netherfield would never have accepted his sister's behaviour. She walked across the room to give him a comforting hug and to kiss him. "Don't worry. If she is half as happy as we are, she will be fine."

The End

AUTHOR'S NOTE:

I hope you enjoyed *Accepting Mr. Darcy.* I have always wondered what would happen if Elizabeth accepted Darcy's first proposal – how they would work through their differences. And I always wondered what Georgiana was thinking.

I have more *Pride and Prejudice* Variations available:

Darcy Unmasked
Darcy At Last
Much Ado about Darcy
Master of Pemberley
Bewitching Mr. Darcy (a sweet Paranormal)
Darcy's Winter Wedding
An Heir for Pemberley

For those of you that are interested, I also write sweet quirky romances under the name Beverly Farr.

To learn about upcoming Darcy stories, please go to my website www.janegrix.com and sign up for my reader's group.

Finally, I love to hear from my readers. You can email me at jane.grix.author@gmail.com or leave a review where you bought this book.

Thanks.

Happy reading,
Jane